Roofing with a Naked Lady and other stories

◆

Roofing with a Naked Lady and other stories

Fred Anderson

Writers Club Press
San Jose New York Lincoln Shanghai

Roofing with a Naked Lady and other stories

Writers Club Press
an imprint of iUniverse, Inc.

For information address:
iUniverse, Inc.
5220 S 16th, Ste. 200
Lincoln, NE 68512
www.iuniverse.com

Cover Design and graphics:
Martha Anderson
Lothair Inc.
13168 Olde Western Avenue
Blue Island Il 60406

ISBN: 0-595-18863-X

Printed in the United States of America

THANK YOU, JERRY

I'd like to thank Jerry Delap for his help with this book. Jerry is a pilot, a flight instructor, and our school psychologist. Each time I told one of my stories at the lunch table, Jerry would look at me as if I were crazy and ask, "What's wrong with you, Anderson?"

I know that Jerry was trying to "put me down" in front of my friends, but his sarcastic question helped me put my stories in perspective and analyze what I really wanted to say.

I do want to thank Jerry for his support when I was learning to fly. He lent me books, helped me through my first solo cross-country flight, and gave me the aluminum lap board that holds my charts and flight plans. Jerry and I found some common ground.

Contents

◆

Foreword

◆

WHAT MAKES FRED DIFFERENT

So he wants to write a book, Fred Anderson tells me.

This is not exactly a statement I have never heard before. That is because I have written books. Therefore people routinely say to me, "I want to write a book," or "I should write a book," or "I could write a book," or "I really ought to write a book." After all, they have had uniquely bookworthy experiences: Joe once talked to a barber who cut the hair of Carmen Basilio's cousin. Sally's psychic predictions, determined by the careful study of shed cat hair on the sofa and ancient Aztec gibberish, always come true sometimes. Herb is one of the few people alive who knows the details of the international conspiracy that has brought on widespread acceptance of tire rotation.

What makes Fred different is that he had actually written something. Pages of something. Most of the "want, should, could," and "ought to" folks somehow never actually get around to putting words on paper, an act which just might be essential for the creation of a book.

So I read the pages of something.

And then–

Yes? asks Fred.

And then–

Okay, let's see how I can say it…Diplomacy and all.

Yes? asks Fred.

No.

No? says Fred.

Not a book. Sorry, Fred. It has the *potential* to be a book. Like, see the bunch of metal over there? That has the *potential* to be a car. That tree? Has the potential to be a table.

Well, then, how do I make it live up to its potential and be a book?

Simple. You learn to write.

Now, *simple* is *not* a synonym for easy. Acquiring the skills to transfer the content of your head and your heart and perhaps that elusive abstraction we call a soul onto a sheet of paper takes a lot of time and a lot of effort. This just might be why so few of the above-mentioned "want, should, could," and "ought to" people abandon their unwritten/never to be written book ideas and instead opt for cross-stitching or a large screen TV with all the WWF pay-per-views or the time share condo in somewhat glorious Lima, Ohio.

Okay, says Fred Anderson, he will learn to write. Seems doable.

In reviewing the manuscript Fred had created, I offered numerous suggestions and commentary meant to guide Fred in his education as a writer.

One must be subtle in one's teaching approach. One must strive to enlighten the student without hurting his self-esteem. One must gently hint, mildly criticize, cautiously explain.

So Fred received such insightful literary comments as:

Don't you trust your reader? You don't have to spell it all out. People who can and do choose to read are not dumb, so don't insult them by treating them as though they were dumb.

Creativity is fine but not when it comes to definitions. Get your dictionary.

Why should this matter to the reader? Before you can answer that, you'd better figure out why it matters to you.

It's a writer's job to choose the exact right words that will mean just and only what he/she means—those words and not the "almost right words."

The reader doesn't know what you're saying here. I doubt that you know what you're saying here.

And of course there is that beginning writer's error which is so easy to spot:

This is stupid. Hoo, boy! Stupid! Man-whoo! Stupid!

And now we come to it: part of the particular *what* that makes Fred different.

Fred did not take up cross-stitching or finance an 82" TV or investigate real estate in Lima, Ohio. He did not join the company of the "want, should, could," and "ought to" people.

He put in the time and effort.

He worked really hard.

He learned to write.

And he has written a good book.

It's called *Roofing with a Naked Lady and Other Stories*, and this it.

Mort Castle
October 18, 2000

Preface

◆

WHO, WHO, WHO WROTE THE BOOK OF FRED?

Fred Anderson has a Master's Degree in the Science of Education from Chicago State University. He is the father of two grown children, Neil Anderson and Lori Ritter, and the grandfather of Justin and Brandon Ritter. He lives with his first and last wife, Joan, on "Septic Acres," a small farm in Indiana. (Don't worry, Fred will explain that name soon!) He and Joan have raised horses, broken a few horses to saddle and a few of their own bones in the process. They have bred cats and dogs and currently raise rabbits in Joan's custom designed rabbitry.

Fred is a songwriter and musician. He has lost his shirt promoting and producing rock and roll, country, folk, and acid rock concerts (Nickel Rebate Productions). He has taught guitar, theater lighting design, leather work, metal work, drafting, auto mechanics, woodworking, cabinet making, pattern making, and construction trades. He has studied Karate, Kung Fu, and Judo and is a perpetual student pilot. He has a bunch of gold crowns in his head and pays his taxes on time. He wishes to be known for his sense of fair play, he wishes it *to be known* that he loves his wife and children and he wishes it to be *widely* known and *publicly declared* that he went to work each morning with enthusiasm.

—The Author
Fred, who else?

Acknowledgements

———————————◆———————————

Special Thanks To:

Joan Anderson

Martha Anderson

Neil Anderson

Cynthia Jacobs

Terri Lacy

Kathy Luther

Arthur Naebig

Mary Crowley

Don Deakin

Joan Deakin

Peggy Demske

Patricia Donnegan

Sheila Elkhern

Joan Gamble

Mort Castle

Dora Cellini

Sue Condon

Nan Connors

Don Croarkin

Ellen Okoniewski

Robin Reising

Lori Ritter

Jeff Schaeffer

Dale Swafford

Judy Swafford

Drew Wickham

Karen Yates

In Memory

◆

These souls hold a place in my mind and my heart. They contribute to these stories and have enriched my life.

Barny 1956
Matu, Freida Potter Lehman 1967
Brother Paul Anderson 1968
Jessie James 1970
Buck 1977
Mackie Jefferson 1981
Terri 1982
Mother, Lillian Anderson 1984
Dad, Fred O Anderson 1989
Lillian Swanson 1991
Caroline Fries 1995
Fred Mercer 1996
Al Versypt 1997
Clayton Moore 1999

Introduction

◆

If you write a book about Fred Anderson, my friend and editor, Mort Castle told me, you might be able to sell a few copies, but only if you stand on a street corner and are very persuasive. Write about the wonderfully amazing and "off the wall" students you have taught, he advised. Write about the fascinating and eccentric adults you have worked with.

It was hard to separate my life from the lives of the people I wrote about, especially when I discovered I was right up there with the craziest of them all. So you will find more than a little "Fred" sprinkled throughout the book.

While I have changed some names, to protect the innocent, the guilty, or their feelings, these stories are true. Although dates are not used, the stories start in 1963, run through 2000, and are arranged in chronological order.

I should also tell you that in many ways, kids have not changed. In the three and a half decades that I've been their teacher, counselor, friend, and sometimes watchman, I've seen that yesterday's and today's young people share the same ambitions, concerns, and funny ways of looking at life.

Kids are still kids.

And teachers are still teachers.

Locked in

◆

"Don't you *dare* lock Dwight inside that storeroom!" I told Bart Johnson. He had the door blocked with his foot. The padlock was in his hand, and he was ready to drop it in the hasp.

"Don't make such a big deal out of it, Mr. Anderson," Bart said. His foot hadn't moved. The kid always needed to be told twice.

"If you put that lock in the hasp, I'll put *you*…out of here! Move your foot away from the door and let Dwight out!"

"You don't have to get so mad," Bart said, taking his foot away from the door.

Dwight slipped out of the storeroom. "We were just playing, Mr. Anderson," he said.

Why do *I get so crazy every time this happens?* I wondered. Perhaps I'm irritated with myself for forgetting to lock the storeroom, or at least forgetting to snap the lock shut on the open hasp so it cannot be used as a pin. Why do I get so emotional every time this scene plays out?

My mind drifted back to Lindbloom Technical High School, one of my first teaching assignments. There, I inadvertently locked two boys and a girl in my lumber storage area.

The three hid in a ventilator shaft, out of sight, emerging the next morning when I unlocked the door.

Disheveled, and looking the worse for wear, they stumbled into the hallway and disappeared around the corner so quickly I didn't have a chance to find out who they were—or if they'd had a good time before they found themselves locked in—or after.

No one ever investigated the incident, or asked me why I locked the kids inside. Just to be on the safe side, I practiced answering the question that never came, "How could you have locked them up over night?"

I stone-faced into the mirror and answered, "I didn't know they were in there…How could I know they were in there…? Why do you assume it was me…? What storeroom?"

My mind drifted back still more, back to when I was a student in high school, to the day Davie Schwartz went berserk in class. That day his classmates locked him away, to hide him from the teacher.

Schwartz always was a little…different. That day in shop class, when Mr. Blinkman, our teacher, (of course, *Blinky* was the unimaginative name we had given him) took off for his usual cigarette break, Schwartz went into his act.

He buzzed about the shop looking for inspiration, then zeroed in on Blinky's desk. After rifling through the papers on top, Schwartz went a step beyond: He opened Blinky's unlocked desk drawers.

The small group watching began to cheer him on. Schwartz rummaged through the drawer's contents. When he found nothing of value, he dumped everything on the floor.

Boy, Blinky is going to be pissed off, I thought. Blinkman sure kept a lot of junk in those drawers.

Schwartz grasped a screwdriver—Blinky's *favorite* screwdriver—with a metal shank running through the handle and pried open Blinky's large locked drawer. A few of the kids in class began to chant, "Go Schwartz. Go Schwartz, go, *go*, GO!!!"

Schwartz went. He moved to the tool cabinet. He pulled out a handsaw, then threw Blinky's chair upside down on the work bench. He chopped four inches from one of the chair legs, then replaced the chair under Blinky's desk. The small group watching, got larger; the volume of chanting increased, "Go Schwartz. Go Schwartz! Go! Go! Go!"

This was getting interesting, as good as a movie. I watched Schwartz pick up a pair of pliers, then remove the drain plug from the door check mounted above the door. Oil blurped on the floor. The entire class was Schwartz's audience now, and they roared with super-charged enthusiasm. Me, too.

"Go Schwartz. Go Schwartz, Go Schwartz, GO GO GO!"

Schwartz retrieved a diagonal side cutters from the tool panel. He chased through the room and cut the plug from the engine lathe, from the drill press, and the small band saw. The group chanted louder and louder. Our joined voices rang, "*GO SCHWARTZ. GO SCHWARTZ, GO, GO, GO!*"

Schwartz was on fire now; he was wound up and cranking. He had the whole team behind him. He was a doer, the great leader, the Mother of Destruction! The kid took Blinky's metal shank screwdriver and pried open the locked fuse box. Sparks shot out in all directions as the blade found the lug screws. 220 volts surged through the metal shank, through Schwartz's body, and out through the bottom of his shoes.

Schwartz trembled, and flipped on his back to the floor. Dazed, he sat up, then looked up at the box.

"Yeah, Schwartz, that was neat."

"That was great."

"Super job, Schwartz," the class cried.

Schwartz was our new hero. He had carried the ball. He had taken a 220 volt shock and he was *still alive*. Looking around at all he had done, he picked himself up from the floor and shook himself off. "I got to get out of here," he said. He knew Blinky would return, and the great adventure would be over.

"We'll hide you, Schwartz," one of the kids said. "Get inside that new tool cabinet, and we'll hide you inside."

The new cabinet had been delivered the day before. Built from unfinished oak, it had a large door that raised up and slipped inside a track above the tool storage area. Schwartz jumped inside and the group pulled the door out and down.

George Thomas was one of Schwartz's worst enemies and George just never missed an opportunity to mess with the kid. He grabbed a hammer, some 16 penny nails, and spiked the door shut. Schwartz banged on the cabinet door. He was locked inside and frantic to get out.

Mr. Blinkman showed up at the door. George yelled through the cabinet for Schwartz to be quiet, that Blinky was coming in the room.

And in the room he came. As the door closed behind him, the door check gave one last shot of oil. Blinky turned around and looked at the door check and the oil on the floor. He wiped the back of his neck with his big paw and walked to his desk. Blinky saw that pried open drawer. He saw his stuff on the floor. He sat on his three legged chair and it fast-tilted forward. His elbow and forearm caught his forward movement to stabilize him. For a moment he surveyed the room.

We were silent. Blinky stared at the class. Mr. Blinkman asked, his voice slower than usual and his words deliberate, "What happened here?" He paused, and within that moment of silence, Schwartz began banging, drumming on the new cabinet from his place inside.

Mr. Blinkman asked again, this time louder and even slower than before, "Just what happened here?" He wanted an answer, now, as he discovered his brand-new, solid-oak cabinet, splintered up and down the two sides where the 16 penny nails were driven through. Mr. Blinkman was very mad. All in all, it was not a good day for Blinkman.

And that is how I learned about kids locking kids up in places. That is why I lock my padlocks back on the open door. That is why I check a room over carefully before locking it up for the night. You just never know.

The Jerk

———————————— ◆ ————————————

"I will not leave your classroom until I am good and ready!" the well dressed man told me. "You would be smart to go about your business. I plan to stay right here."

I was a new teacher at Lindbloom Technical High School. The Principal, Harry Yates, had asked me to keep an eye on the hallways and to remove any adult from the building who would not show his identification as a school employee or visitor. Now this stranger had walked into my shop classroom, was standing against the wall, and wouldn't leave.

I had walked over to him while the class was working and introduced myself. I asked if I could help him, but he told me he was just looking around. I asked if he belonged in the building, and he said that he certainly did. I asked to see his identification, and he looked at me, then said, "If you don't know who I am, you had better learn."

I did not like his attitude, especially when he snapped, "I don't have to show you identification. You better find out just who I am."

Enough is enough! I thought, and *besides, my students are watching. It's showdown time in room 128!* I picked up a 3" x 3" x 36" hardwood furniture square that leaned between the two wood lathes, next to where our visitor stood. I whacked it down flat on the work bench. It cracked resoundingly. It was a definite attention-getter. It caught the attention of the well dressed man and the attention of every kid in the room.

I moved toward him with the club; he started toward the door.

6

"I'm going to the office!" he shouted, looking over his shoulder.

"You're going outside!" I shouted back. "You're going outside, or I'll split your head open!" I walked him out of my classroom, down the hallway, out the side door of the building, and then pulled the crashbar tight. When I returned, I knew I had moved to a higher level on the student-teacher pecking order; the kids thought I was great.

Later that day, I got a note to see Principal Yates before I went home. He began by saying, "You had no right throwing the District Superintendent out of my building," I felt the blood drain from my head. "But, you said to…"

"I was talking about drunks, not the District Superintendent!"

My legs felt wobbly, I looked for a chair. "But he came into my room and…"

"You had better behave yourself in the future, Anderson," Principal Yates continued. "You're new here. That man was in your classroom to evaluate your teaching!" Sitting down was not a good idea now. Falling down probably wasn't, either.

Principal Yates was waving me out the door.

I was rethinking my position in the pecking order, as I called my father that evening, and told him the story. Dad had been in the school business in Chicago for years, and seemed to know everyone.

"Your evaluation won't be great, but you'll survive," he said. "Maybe next time, that son-of-a-gun, Sullivan, will ask permission to go into a classroom. He might even have the good sense to introduce himself."

"Then you do remember him, Dad?"

"Yes, I remember him," my father said. "Sullivan and I went to school together. I remember him; the guy was always a jerk."

The Jaguar Mark VII

The Jaguar Mark VII I drove to my first teaching assignment had a sun roof, high backed leather seats, Circassian walnut dash, bud vases mounted on each side of the door posts, and two fuel tanks. A dash panel switch allowed the driver to select one of two leaky electric fuel pumps. The pumps often needed repair and the tanks they drew from alternately required patching. When I could match the combination of a good fuel pump with a good fuel tank, I could drive the car from home to work and from gas station to gas station.

Gas mileage was not the best.

I loved the car from the moment I saw it; it was my first car. My father helped me tow it home from the used car dealership on the end of a strong rope. Without the aid of a running motor and power steering I fought the car around corners. Without power brakes it was a trick to keep the tow rope taut. I pushed the brake pedal with both feet to slow the car and to keep the Jaguar from running up on the tow vehicle, the family station wagon.

The Jaguar's big motor had a rod knock and the front left fender was smashed. The dealer promised a new fender was on order from England, but my dad said it would probably never come.

We spent the winter working on the car, sometimes in sub-zero weather and in deep snow. My dad showed me how to take the engine apart, fit the new rod bearings and reassemble it without parts left over. Together we pounded out and remolded the fender. My dad was a good mechanic. He was a schemer, a self-made engineer and a teacher. I did most of the work, but he showed me how to machine unavailable parts and helped me fix my mistakes. We worked together long hours. I learned patience from him, an important teaching skill I strive to use today. The Jaguar helped me know my father far better than I had known him before.

The Jaguar resembled an older Rolls Royce. The car was shining and elegant; it looked important. Gary, a black friend of mine, asked me to pick him up after work where he pumped gas at his uncle's service station. He wanted me to drive him around his neighborhood. Gary sat in the back while I wore a hat and played his chauffeur. He acted his role well, called out and waved to his friends.

One day we took a chance. Gary and I drove the Jaguar down the Dan Ryan Expressway before the road was opened. We pulled up to a barricaded entrance, moved the sawhorse aside and made our prelimi-nary run on the same day that Chicago's mayor, Richard M. Daley, was to tour the newly constructed highway. We drove without traffic on the new white pavement, dodging stacks of concrete form materials and empty barrels as they waited for last minute pick-up. I felt like a big wheel in my Jaguar. I was the King of the Road.

Then the King ran out of pavement. The road ended downtown; it exited into at least half the Chicago Police Department waiting for Mayor Daley's parade to start.

I knew we were in for it now. I pulled up to the barricaded exit. I had broken out in a cold sweat and my hands were shaking as I rolled down the window. In the most official voice I could command, I asked two of the officers to move the saw horse. I told them we needed to make the return run, and without hesitation they opened the exit and then the entrance for my Jaguar. Sometimes a little bluff goes a long way.

I courted my wife Joan in the Jaguar. She sometimes rode with her head and shoulders through the open sun roof as she sat on top the seat's back. I fell in love with her in the car. The purple lights on the dash set a wonderful mood at night. We broke up in the car and I drove around sadly for months until we reconciled.

I learned some things about reverse discrimination in the Jaguar. One evening, just before dusk, I went over to the gas station to visit Gary and load the one good tank with gas. I paid for the fuel with a twenty and as the bill changed from my hand to Gary's a gust of wind tore it away. The bill blew to the ground. Both of us made a move to pick it up, but before we reached it, the wind picked it up and carried it down a side street away from the busy intersection.

Gary left the pumps and helped me chase down the bill. The money flew up in a tree and fluttered back down again where it skidded across the sidewalk. It blew with the wind for a block and a half. Gary and I chased it through his all-black neighborhood.

I grabbed the bill, then someone grabbed me. Gary's neighbors had watched Gary running after me. They left their porches to help with the capture.

I drove my Jaguar limousine for four wonderful years but came to realize I was underneath fixing things more than I was driving the car. I lay on my back in my good clothes rebuilding a fuel pump in the Grant Park Underground Garage while my date waited patiently to go home from a play. I spent two weeks in Wisconsin with brake parts on order from New York and fished for bluegills until they arrived.

My dad fell so in love with the car that he found and bought another. For a while we had a pair and rebuilt our cars together. It broke my heart to sell the Jaguar Mark VII but I could not afford the time nor money to pamper her through her unreliable moods.

I traded the elegant Jaguar for a Fiat.

The Fiat was reliable transportation.

It was not pretentious.

It was lacking in style.

It was a tin can.

Driving to work was never the same.

Please Excuse Fred, He is Late to Work

◆

Sometimes my students are late. They always have an excuse.

This is my pedagogical response:

I have driven three Fiats to work, a Jaguar limousine, an Edsel, a Dodge van, two Chevy vans, three Ford vans, a Cadillac, Plymouth, three Ford sedans, a Taurus, Pontiac, two Oldsmobile and three Chevy station wagons. I have driven two motorcycles, two bicycles, a John Deere Model A farm tractor, walked, ran and ridden to work on horseback. I have been late to work in all these years, four or five times.

I have seen accidents and I have stopped to assist with accidents. I have created accidents and I have been arrested. I have seen airplanes blocking the road as they were being towed from one place to another. I have seen an airplane crashed on the road. I have stopped to rope two or three run-away horses. I have been late to work four or five times.

I have been sick to my stomach, stuck in the snow and stuck in the mud, the dog has run off, our cat had kittens, another dog had puppies, our horse had a foal, the roof leaked, a water main burst in the house, the furnace went out, I broke my foot, I broke my other foot, I broke my nose and my finger and four or five ribs. I have been late to work four or five times.

I have had a flat tire, a dead battery, leaky radiator, wet ignition wires, bad fuel pump, faulty distributor, blown power steering pump, broken fan belt, sticky valves, locked brakes, broken drive shaft and a ruptured coolant hose. I have been late to work four or five times.

Jackie

◆

Jackie Sanderson was a custodian. I got to know Jackie and the rest of the cleaning crew during the summer months when I worked with the men cleaning the building. I had begun teaching at Bloom's Freshman-Sophomore Division, and my wife, Joan, and I had bought our small farm that year, named it with good reason "Septic Acres," and the summer work helped pay for very necessary sewer work. Pushing my scaffolding, ladder, and cleaning equipment around, I washed every window in the school, inside and out. Even though I was a school teacher, I was eventually accepted by the custodial guys and made to feel part of the group.

Jackie Sanderson had stories and it didn't take long to get him started during the morning coffee break. I arranged my window cleaning schedule around Jackie, and where his room scrubbing crew were working, so that I could join him during the break for "Sanderson's Story Time."

"Tell me more about Al Capone, Jackie," I would ask, as I flopped down on the floor with my thermos of coffee.

"I shined Al Capone's shoes. Did I ever tell you that?" he asked. "I had a shoe shine stand at the racetrack. Capone would get up in the high chair. His men would stand around while I shined his shoes. I'd spit on my hands, make that rag pop and snap. I could put on a real shine. Mr. Capone was a real gent, called me by name. He always tipped me real good and once gave me a 50 dollar bill. That was the biggest tip I ever got. Fifty dollars. Ain't that somethin'?

"Later I worked for the organization," he said. "We hid liquor inside the loads of lumber on the lumber trucks. Some of them companies that deals with the school helped move the booze around.

"I always did good work," Jackie said. "Pretty soon I got to drive the trucks and I made the deliveries myself."

"Did you ever get to see some action, Jackie?" I asked.

"Just once," he answered. "And I got real scared. I was delivering beer in the Heights to a place where we were having some problems. I carried in a small keg. It was still on my shoulder when two men busted in with guns. They shot up the place, killed the owner and someone else behind the bar. One man turned the gun on me and the other said, 'Leave him alone, he works for us.' I set that keg down. I left and never looked back."

Jackie was connected with the political machine and worked at the license bureau. A little of Capone must have rubbed off on him; he always carried large amounts of cash in his pockets and enjoyed flashing it around. "You never know when you might have to buy a little somethin'," he told me. "Some of those peoples at the bureau needs a little help. Some of them folks can't read or write, Fred. They pays me a little to help them with the test and the paper work. They needs that license to drive and get back and forth to work."

"Do you get to keep the money?" I asked in ignorance.

"Just my cut," he said, "just my share."

With summer winding down, I took the last week off and when I returned to start teaching, I visited the cleaning crew.

Jackie wasn't with them.

"He's had an accident, Fred," one of the guys explained. "He took a fall and got hurt pretty bad."

I asked, "How did it happen?"

"He was changing light bulbs in the girl's gym, using the scaffolding you used this summer. It was extended several tiers higher so he could reach the ceiling. The two kids hired to help him started playing grab ass. One kid chased the other and grabbed the post as he made the corner. They pulled the scaffold out from under Jackie. We figure he fell about 24 feet. He grabbed the unit on his way down, probably slowed his fall, but it all came down on top of him."

"Did he get hurt bad?" I wanted to know.

"Broken hip, broken ribs, one twisted-up wrist. His wife says he hurts real bad."

"What happened to the kids who did this to him?"

"Goddamn kids," he said. "They said they were sorry, continued to work that last week and screw around like they did all summer. You know, that shouldn't be allowed."

I saw Jackie several months later. He came back for a visit. He limped and said it hurt when he walked or sat. "I'm not doing too well," he told me. "The doctor says somethin's wrong with my prostate."

I studied him. He had shrunk down in size. His skin was hanging differently, and had lost its healthy brown tone. His eyes were different.

I had a feeling I was visiting with him for perhaps the last time.

"I hope you feel better," I told him. "I enjoyed talking with you this past summer, Jackie. And thanks for telling me about Al Capone."

"I shined Al Capone's shoes," he said. "Did I ever tell you that?"

Barry And I Size Each Other up

———————— ◆ ————————

I read my evaluation, and as the words began to sink in, I broke into a cold sweat. The evaluation should have been a formality, after all I was not a first year teacher. I had come to Bloom Township High School after working in Chicago and had settled into the Freshman-Sophomore Division with enthusiasm. But this evaluation questioned my methods of working with lower ability students. It attacked my classroom management techniques and this man who wrote it, this man who talked in a western drawl, was even critical of my Midwestern speech patterns. I continued reading the report in disbelief.

I had worked hard to provide kids with a good education and I felt I was doing a good job, but there was Mr. Fields's report, three pages of educational garble. It focused on areas of weakness, areas I knew were my strengths. The evaluation he had written had nothing good to say.

Mr. Fields, the assistant principal, had been in my room to visit. He had come in unannounced, walked around for five minutes and then left. At the end of the day he called me into his office, and when I sat down, handed me the evaluation of my teaching.

"I can't sign this!" I said, realizing I was flying in the face of his authority. Our relationship had been formal and cordial, but as soon as I made the statement, I knew things would never be the same.

"What do you mean you won't sign it?" he challenged me.

"I don't agree with it," I answered. "I do not agree with *anything* you have said. There's a lot at stake here, and you weren't in my classroom long enough to have properly observed me."

I could feel him study me. He pushed his chair a few inches back from his desk, then paused before he spoke. "What do you want me to do?" he asked.

"Find something good to say. I really enjoy working at Bloom and want to continue. Rewrite the thing and I'll sign it. Could you do that, Mr. Fields?" I asked.

"Call me Barry," he said, then retrieved the evaluation. "I'll look my work over and see you in an hour."

Mr. Fields must have been under some deadline, because he found me before the hour was up. He had rewritten the evaluation, and it was glowing. I felt relieved and signed it quickly, before he changed his mind. Barry Fields and I moved on to a new level.

Barry was the assistant principal, but originally had been an English teacher and before that a blacksmith from Wyoming; he knew something about teaching and shop work. As I got to know him, he became a father figure and eventually my friend. I worked hard trying to please the man and fit his idea of what a teacher should be.

Barry was in charge of buses and school security. I worked after school under his direction. I loaded the buses, supervised the halls during the activity period, then checked to see that classrooms were empty and locked each afternoon. The racial tension mounting in the school compromised the safety of the students and the staff. Separating students who were fighting and keeping theft and vandalism in check were part of my duties. It was during this period that Barry and I were invited to train in a self-defense program with the police department. We joined their class in Kung Fu and trained on hardwood floors; the luxury of mats was not part of the discipline.

Barry was twenty-five years older than I, but the muscles in his arms and legs had never lost their blacksmith hardness. He stood eight inches taller than I and outweighed me by 80 pounds. He was fast, his movements cat-like and although he tempered his blows and kicks as we sparred, there were times he hurt me. I learned to stand my ground and fight him toe to toe. The punishment he inflicted upon my smaller body only served to heighten the sense of accomplishment I felt each time I threw my boss on his back on those hardwood floors.

Barry came home with me to Septic Acres on several occasions to help me with some horse training. It was here I learned how strong he really was. He walked out into the horse paddock and spent some time talking to Terry, one of Joan's mares. When the mare quieted down, he positioned himself under her body, straightened up and lifted her off the ground. She dangled over Barry's shoulders, her front legs thrashing, her hoofs feeling for the ground. He then set her down.

"How did you do that, Barry?" I asked, more concerned with Terry's rib cage than with the answer.

"I started picking up one of my horses in Wyoming when it was just born and weighed a few hundred pounds," he said. "Each day I picked the foal up as it gained weight, until the day it was full grown. Now, once in a while, I pick up a horse just to keep in practice."

I studied him for a moment and evaluated his logic. "Barry, I can see your idea worked with a horse," I said, "but would it work with an elephant?"

The Vagabond Lounge

◆

Bloom Township High School hosted a countywide meeting of Industrial Arts teachers. When the formal meeting was over, the group toured a few of our local industries. We later arranged for one more tour. We took our guests to the "Vagabond Lounge" where the show girls danced their clothes away. It was a nice place. You could relax with an artistic presentation and enjoy an eight dollar bottle of Budweiser.

Some of the men from the north side of Chicago didn't get home until the next day; the girls were willing to work long past closing time and into the next morning.

The meeting was remembered for years as the best all-around stress-releasing meeting of all.

Willie Williams And the
Roachy Radio

◆

"Can you fix my radio?" Willie Williams asked.

"This is *woodshop*, Willie," I told him. "We work with wood in woodshop."

"I know, Mr. Anderson," he said, "but you can fix anything."

I looked at Willie Williams in his shabby clothes and I looked at his portable radio. You could bet that, no matter how reasonably priced, you would not find radio replacement money in the pockets of Williams's worn jeans.

I might be able to fix it, I thought. The repair might not be too complicated, maybe something that only required soldering. And sure enough, when Willie's class left the room and I had time to myself, I opened the radio and found a broken connection. After the simple repair, I popped in a few fresh batteries and *Voila!*, music and scratchy sounds from far away places filled the room. Would the short wave bands pick up aircraft communications? I wondered. My small farm, Septic Acres, lies under an aircraft holding area. I would take the radio home to find out.

The outside temperature was below zero, and the heater in the Chevy pickup wasn't working. The doors were leaky, and there were holes in the floor boards. The truck was a wind break at best, and the ride home was cold. When I arrived, I forgot to bring the radio inside. It stayed in the frigid truck until I remembered to bring it in just before I went to bed. I fiddled with the radio for awhile, couldn't hear an airplane, then put it back in the truck so I would not forget it in the morning.

Willie Williams was not in school the next day; his radio warmed up on my desk. When he returned, I took him into my office and opened the radio to show the repairs. *Where did these small extra wires come from?* my mind questioned, *and why are they moving?*

There, between the circuit board and the radio case, were scores of little feelers.

"Geez, Willie!" I cried. "Where did all these cockroaches come from?"

"Probably my house," he answered. "They like to get in places and hide."

"But there's a whole herd of them in there, Willie," I said. "Your radio is crawling with roaches!"

What a piece of luck, I thought, as Willie retrieved his radio. Those bugs were in some cold induced hibernation, too sleepy to invade my home.

Willie thanked me for the repairs, then several days later rewarded me with another radio to fix.

"No, thanks, Willie," I told him. "Let's put this one in a plastic bag. And I think we'll wrap it up tightly, *real* tightly, and you can take it home."

Roasting Sparrows O'ER an Open Fire

───────────────── ◆ ─────────────────

"Now you've gone too far, Anderson," English teacher Richard Nolan told me, as we sipped early morning coffee in the faculty lounge. "I was believing some of that other stuff, but you'll have to go a long way to get me to believe this one."

Richard and I were sharing hunting stories. My story was about my childhood. It didn't seem too much out of the ordinary. I hadn't told a big whopper, but Richard was questioning my story. He was *threatening* my credibility.

Oh, Richard had believed me when I told him I had become just too good with a gun; the thrill of the hunt and killing game was over for me, now that I was an adult. I told Richard that I'd started to hunt when I was very young. My younger brother, Paul, and I hunted almost every day after school: pigeons, sparrows, rats, raccoons, opossums, ground-hogs, chipmunks—nearly anything that crawled or flew. Paul and I hunted in forest preserves, backyards, and in the cemetery. We broke our rifles down, then concealed the parts inside our pants in the cloth holsters my grandmother sewed on her foot-treadle sewing machine. The pouches held the gun barrel down one leg and the stock down the other. We walked stiff-legged through the Chicago South Side neighborhood to the hunting grounds.

Richard believed me when I told him there were times Paul and I were chased by the police. We hobbled away as if our legs were encased in immovable casts. The cops never chased us far; they must have

22

thought the crippled stiff-legged boys were not the boys with the guns they were looking for.

Richard believed me, too, when I told him our hunting friend, Jimmie Alex, held the key to his family crypt. We hunted the cemetery for ground squirrels and would enter the locked tomb for shelter or to hide from the cemetery workers.

I told Richard we were once cornered by the cemetery workers and hid the guns away, then wept over an open grave. The men questioned us about hunting and Jimmie went into his act. He looked up to the sky and asked why we weren't allowed to be left alone, in our grief, to bury our dead. The men finally left, unsure if we were really left over from the funeral. Jimmie went on to become a lawyer. Richard Nolan had no problem with the story.

Richard believed me when I told him that when hunting was poor, we sometimes shot sparrows for a meal, then roasted them over an open fire. "It takes a lot of those little birds to make a meal," I told him. "Not much meat on a sparrow."

But then I told him how we caught big bumble bees, held them down and removed their stingers with a pair of long nose pliers. "The bees will live for a while without their stingers," I said. "We'd tie a very light weight thread around one little leg and fly our bees around on their tethers."

It was this story that was too much for Richard Nolan. At this point his belief system just broke down.

I would have to do something quickly, to reestablish his trust in me, and so I went to the faculty pay phone to call my mother in Chicago. "Mom," I said to her, "do you remember when we pulled the stingers out of bumble bees? Would you explain to a friend of mine, here at school, what we did? He doesn't believe me."

And so my mother reestablished my reputation, and told Richard how we flew the bees around on their little leashes. When Richard hung up the phone, he said, "Fred, your mother verified your story, but to be honest, I think your mother is even a better story teller than you are."

Snow Shoes

◆

I slipped the toes of my boots into the sheet metal toe straps of my homemade show shoes, screwed the plywood bottoms to my boot heels and put the red handled screwdriver in my back pocket. The blizzard had snowed me in at school for two days now. I was getting edgy; it was time to go home.

Joan was seven months pregnant. The day the snow began to fall was to be her last day teaching in Beecher, Illinois. I was worried about her and our baby she was carrying. I hoped she was safe. If she was stranded too, no one would be home at Septic Acres. Our horses would be locked in the barn, hungry and thirsty. The cats would need food and our poor dog, in need of a walk, ready to explode.

I looked out the window towards the parking lot one more time. Snow had blown over the cars and although I knew where I had parked the old Plymouth, it was swallowed up and had disappeared along with the other cars in the row.

I adjusted my fuzzy ear muffs under the hood of my jacket, then zipped up. At least I'm dressed for the walk, I thought, pulling the lined mittens over my hands. Bob Murphy, the man I was to travel with, helped me open the door. Together we pushed and battered the snow away. I thought about the warm school and the friends I was leaving behind.

All the kids were out of the building, thanks to "super driver" Diane Johnson. She had driven her school bus back to Bloom High School three times and picked up the last waiting routes. I physically pushed four kids out into the snow and onto Diane's bus. They insisted on waiting for rides I knew would never come.

Hope she makes it, I thought as I watched Diane blast out of the driveway one last time. Snow sprayed over the top of her bus, as she dodged the stranded cars abandoned in the roadway. Teachers were relieved; we wouldn't have to baby sit.

I took a head count. There were 15 of us left behind. One custodian was stuck with us. He kept the boilers fired. The school cook couldn't get her car to move. She unlocked the kitchen and showed us where she kept the leftovers. We would have more than enough to eat.

We assembled in the music room the first evening, to organize a songfest, but found that the music director, snowed in with the rest of us, had earlier quarreled with our piano player. Mr. Music Director locked the sheet music away, then locked the piano and refused to let anyone play.

I didn't see any point in arguing, not when I could resolve the disagreement with a hammer and screwdriver. I operated on the locks, and although I promised to repair the splintered cover on the piano where the wood held the hasp, the music director screamed at me, then disappeared into some recess of the building where he remained throughout the storm.

Most of the group had retired that night to the P.E. area. They bedded down on gym mats and on trampolines, and covered themselves with jackets and coats. I slept in my shop storeroom. I dumped a 50 pound bale of clean multi-colored shop rags on the floor, fluffed them around and burrowed in for the night. I lay in the dark, organizing the way I would fix the splintered piano. I wondered where the music director had gone. I worried about Joan's safety and the safety of our unborn baby. I wished Joan were there; I wanted to share my bed of rags. I thought about our animals, neglected now for too long. I tried to remember that long stretch of woods between school and my home, and before I fell asleep, I visualized how I would make my snow shoes, how I would attach them to my boots and what route I would take to go home.

Before I fell asleep, I had a plan.

Early the next morning a cold, tired man stumbled into the building. I was putting the finishing touches on my snow shoes when Bob Murphy found me working in the shop. "How you doin'," he started, introducing himself. "It took me two hours to walk the mile down the road from the Ford Stamping Plant. After I get warm, I'm startin' out again for home. Here, let me help you with those toe straps," he continued. "I'm a sheet metal worker at Ford. Think those things will keep you on top of the snow? What are them bolts stickin' down? Spikes? Will it keep you from slidin'? Don't know if it'll work. Whatcha think? Maybe just your boot'll work better. You live in Dyer? You should go right past my house. When you get ready to go, I'll walk with you; gotta get home. My wife'll be waitin'. Got a mess of kids at home. Hope they're warm and all right."

I calculated, using Bob's time and distance information, that I'd never make it home in boots, but the snowshoes worked well. I walked on top of the snow while Bob sank with every step. We looked for places where the wind had chiseled the snow to its lowest depth but we were often fooled. I spent a lot of energy pulling him out of snowdrifts.

"Them snow shoes seem to work pretty good," he said. It was a sharp observation that came from a man stuck in a drift up to his chin.

We walked against the wind toward the expressway. The traffic light cycled from red to green but did nothing to encourage the cars and trucks abandoned and wedged in the drifts. We pushed on toward Bob's house down the side streets of Sauk Village. Three hours had passed and I could see Bob was tired as he finally climbed his porch steps. "Come on in," he said. He pulled open the door and motioned to me with his free hand. "You come on in and get warm for awhile."

Bob's wife stood in the darkened doorway. My eyes fought to adjust from the bright outdoors to see her more clearly. She moved closer to the entrance. Holding a baby in her arms, she was surrounded by the rest of her brood. Small children clutched at her skirt and apron. Her hair pointed in all directions. She looked haggard and explosive.

"Hi, honey," Bob said. "I'm home."

"Where! Just *where* in the Hell have you been! I've been here by myself! Don't you care? Where have you been? Just where in the Hell have you been?"

Bob tried to speak but she cut him off. He tried to explain but it just wasn't working.

Bob fumbled through a hallway cabinet junk drawer and extracted a brass compass. "Here," he said, opening the case and handing it to me, "I use this for deer hunting. Hope it gets you where you need to go." It was clear he was dismissing me.

I backed out the door and felt the cold wind on my sweaty back. It would have been nice to have stayed awhile, gotten warm and dried out, I thought, but inside I could hear the battle rage on. Maybe it wasn't so bad out here, I decided.

Bob's house was at the far end of Sauk Village. His back yard adjoined Rickert's farm field.

I opened the brass case of Bob's compass and took a reading. The sky had darkened, more snow was coming. Without the sun to guide me, Bob's compass would be as important as my snow shoes, I thought as I walked between the fence posts and over the top strand of barb wire buried under the snow.

I started off cross country, away from roads, toward Indiana and my home. The wind had shifted from the south. It was starting to snow again. Heading directly east, I thought about the trip ahead.

The woods lay about two hours off with the river beyond. There I would have to look for a tree that had fallen across the stream, or build a make-shift bridge. The bridge on Steger Road was an hour farther south. If I went there, I'd be backtracking, losing even more time.

The river worried me. I could fall in and get wet. Getting soaked would be more than a discomfort in this situation. Still, I decided to try to find some place ahead to cross the river.

The small cottage, smoke streaming from the chimney, at the forest edge was a welcome sight. I hoped whoever was inside wouldn't be frightened. I knocked on the door. I had been walking a long time and needed to rest and get warm.

A young woman opened her door, and to my relief, said without hesitation, "Looks like you've been out in this stuff for awhile. Come on in." Bonnie Myers introduced herself and then, motioning me to a chair, she asked, "How about some warm soup?" I pulled the red handled screwdriver from my pocket so as not to scratch her chair and sat down.

The cottage was warm and Bonnie Myers seemed as starved for company as I was for her soup. It was a wonderful cup of soup, probably the best of my life, but I left the cottage as soon as I knew I could travel again and headed east.

A half mile into the woods the snow on the ground began to feel different. It was powdery and had fallen in a different consistency as it filtered in between the trees. My snow shoes punched deeper with every step. I could not stay on top as before. Each time I raised my foot now, a block of snow came with it. I sat down to remove the snow shoes and looked back at my trail. Drifting snow erased my footprints and the weather had gotten colder. I felt the layer of moisture in my clothing as I reached for my screwdriver.

The screwdriver was gone. Had I lost it on the trip or had I left it back at the cottage? Without that screwdriver I was trapped in my snowshoes and trapped in the woods. I was too winded to go back, and although the river was just ahead, I needed to rest. I sat in the still woods with all that beautiful snow and I began to get sleepy and cold.

A feeling of aloneness crept over me as the sky grew overcast. I had to carefully balance the need to rest and the need to stay warm. I had to move again or I would freeze. I fought to get up and push towards the river.

For the first time I felt frightened.

My feet were swollen and cold and they hurt. I had been walking for six hours and it had taken me two hours to fight the one half mile through the powdery snow in the woods to the river but there I found logs and branches to build a bridge across the unfrozen open water. With the balance of a tightrope walker—a tired and frightened one!—I made my way across and walked through another farm field where the snow shoes worked well again. The compass heading positioned me close to the intersection of two roads.

I knew exactly where I was. The compass had guided me within 50 feet of where I planned to be.

I wept when I turned in my driveway. My feet were swollen and I had a hard time removing my boots once inside. Our poor dog, Heidi, had held her bowels and bladder for 36 hours. The horses were hungry, thirsty, and restless but had not broken down the stalls. I eventually received a call from Joan. She had caught a train from Beecher into Chicago and was safe with her aunt and uncle.

When Joan returned home the next day, we shared our adventures. "Those snow shoes were the ticket, Joan," I told her. "If I hadn't built them I wouldn't have gotten home."

"Sure you would," she countered. "You should have stayed on the road. You forget, Fred, when you lost your screwdriver, those snow shoes tried to kill you."

The Red Streak

◆

The fight between Dorothy Wells and Donna Banks was brutal. They had torn at each other with their finger nails, and now they were in close, trading fists. Dorothy's face and neck were marked and her shoulders and upper arms scratched. Her blouse hung in shreds. She was wearing no bra and the boys cheering them on were loving it.

I thought I could stop the fight by yelling. I thought I could stop it by getting in between the two of them. Then I saw Sarah Barnes.

She had managed to slip in between me and the action. The knife she pulled from her purse reflected the overhead light in the room. The glare caught my eye; the two girls fighting now seemed less important.

I grabbed Sarah's wrist and she spun to face me. The crowd was in too close to pull her arm with the knife down. I held it in the air as she twisted away, then coiled back towards me, pulling against her captured arm. Sarah reeled back again and this time, as she pulled close, I saw her knee shoot toward my groin.

Pivoting on one foot, I turned and felt her knee brush past my outside leg. That was close, I thought, pulling her to the outside of the crowd, to a place with more room to maneuver. It was here, away from the others, that I threw Sarah on her back and snapped open her clutched hand holding the knife.

I heard the blade skip across the tile floor and come to rest somewhere in the far corner of the cafeteria.

Well, at least that's over, I thought. I relaxed my grip on Sarah's wrist. She lunged and bit me on the hand.

The fight was over now. Another teacher, Bob Nardella, and police officer, Jerry Sill, had the two girls separated, and Sarah had finally calmed down so I could take her through the crowd to the office. I looked down at my wounded hand, then toward the empty corner of the room as we walked out. *Where was that knife? Where did that knife go?*

Sarah's mother came to see the principal within the hour. Her little girl was in serious trouble: It was a police matter now. Sarah had a weapon.

There was also the matter of her being "roughed up." Her mother had seen her bruised wrist and bloodied nose. Sarah was complaining her arm hurt. Where *was* that teacher who made the weapon accusation? Who *was* that teacher who *manhandled* her daughter—who, obviously, had used excessive force?

The meeting with Sarah's mother was not going well. Through the glass I could tell Mrs. Barnes was doing most of the talking. Assistant Principal, Len Hickman, excused himself and met me in the hall.

"Fred, Mrs. Barnes is accusing you of making this knife thing up, to cover the way you restrained Sarah. Do you have any idea what happened to the knife? Did some other student get it, or could it still be down there somewhere? Let's go to the cafeteria and look."

Len and I entered the lunchroom. The chairs had been straightened and the floor in the fight arena freshly mopped. The custodian, wearing rubber gloves, was pushing his wheeled pail down the far side of the room.

"Angelo," I called to him, across the room. "I can see you did some floor cleaning."

"Yeah, the office called and asked me to clean up a blood spill."

"Did you find a knife?" I asked. "One of the kids had a knife, and it would help if we had it now. It disappeared during a fight."

"Didn't see a knife. I'll keep my eyes open," Angelo said, glancing around. "I heard it was a hell of a fight," he added, holding up the sleeve of Dorothy Well's blouse.

"What about inside one of these locked storerooms?" Len Hickman asked. He had stooped down and was looking at the wide slit under the door. "Angelo, could you open these two store rooms?"

"Sure," Angelo replied, walking toward us, "but those rooms always stay locked. You won't find a knife in there…"

"Open them anyway," Len directed.

Angelo fingered through the 100 keys on his huge key ring. He found the correct key, unlocked the door and swung it open.

There it lay on the floor: the eight-inch butcher knife I had seen in Sarah's hand.

Len bent over and picked up the weapon. "I think we can go back to the meeting now. It's time for you to talk to Sarah's mom." Sarah's mother glared at me when Len and I entered. She glared at Len when he began to speak and then she glared again at me, when I was introduced.

Then she looked at the knife when Len set it down on the conference table, and I watched her expression change as he asked her the question: "Mrs. Barnes, have you seen this knife before?"

Her expression further changed as she answered, "Yes, it's mine. I'm missing it from my kitchen."

Then she looked at me—no glare. "What else did she do?" she asked.

"She bit me, Mrs. Barnes," I answered. "She bit me on the hand…"

"Yeah, she bites," said Mrs. Barnes. "Sorry about that."

When I got home, Joan looked at my hand the school nurse had bandaged. "We'll have to keep an eye on that," she said, unwrapping the bandage and reaching for the hydrogen peroxide. "You got too close, didn't you? And one of them bit you. I told you not to get too close…"

It was 11:30, time to turn off the *Tonight Show* and think about bed. Joan had been staring at me on and off as we sat on the couch; what could she want?

"Honey," she said, "we have to get you to a doctor. You have a red streak running up the vein in your arm. You have blood poisoning."

I looked down at my bandaged hand, to the place where Sarah Barnes had bitten me earlier that day. The TV was off now, and Joan had turned on the overhead light. I could see the angry red streak, traces of the blood poisoning Joan had observed in the semi-dark room.

"What if we wait until morning?" I asked. I knew what her answer would be.

"Good idea," she answered, "but they will be calling you 'Stumpy' at work, once you get your hand cut off.

"Do you *really* want to wait until morning," Joan asked, "Stumpy?"

I looked again at the red line running up my arm.

Sometimes, with a little nudge, I can be quite decisive.

Dad's Short Finger

◆

The day before my father came to visit me at Bloom High School, I had given a safety demonstration on the use of the jointer. "Only joint a piece of wood 12 inches long or longer. Be careful where you place your fingers."

Then I told the class the story of my father's short finger. "My dad was using a jointer in his high school class. He knew he was breaking a safety rule, jointing a piece of wood under 12 inches in length," I told them. "He was looking over his shoulder to see if the teacher would catch him. Zap! He cut off part of his finger."

That safety lesson was fresh in my students' minds the next day when the office called. "Mr. Anderson, you have a visitor. Your father is here. Could you send a student down to show him the way?" I sent Richard Salsberry.

It was a treat whenever Dad visited me. I was proud of my shop and the projects the kids were making. I knew Dad was pleased I had followed in his footsteps to become a teacher.

Richard gave my dad a tour of the shop. When it was time to leave, Dad walked over to Richard, shook his hand and thanked him for his help.

I watched Richard slowly rotate my father's hand. He was staring at Dad's fingers.

"Do you know what Richard is doing?" I asked. "He's looking for your short finger…"

Richard Salsberry's face reddened. He looked away from Dad's hand, then looked at the floor. "I'm so embarrassed," he said.

"Come over to the jointer," Dad said to Richard. "I'll show you just how I had the accident..."

"Oh, no!" Richard shot back. "I know how you did it; Mr. Anderson told us all about it. Don't show me," he continued. "You might cut off another finger!"

Chris Cross

◆

Chris and his girlfriend exchanged clothing and went to school. Dean Richardson suspended Chris and Chris's mother called. She was furious.

"My son has the right to freedom of expression," she said. "You had no right to suspend him for the clothing he wore." She went on and on.

When she settled down long enough for Mr. Richardson to get a word in edgewise, he explained, "When your son, Chris, walked into the ladies room to straighten his clothes, he crossed the line."

The UPS And Downs of Vandalism

◆

The emergency bell rang, then rang again; someone was stuck in the elevator.

Some kids must have jumped inside, before the door closed, I thought. They didn't have an issued key, so, sneaking a ride, they got themselves locked inside.

The bell rang again. Now someone was beating on the door, frantic to get out.

"Wait until I find my key," I called, thumbing through my too big key ring. (Teachers have big rings of keys; not necessarily as big as janitors, but big.)

Bang, bang, bang! the pounding continued.

"Hold your horses! I've got to find the key."

I slipped the key in the slot, turned it, and the doors parted. The smell of spray paint greeted my nose, and two kids stumbled out of a blue fog, coughing and hacking.

They'd been in there for more than just a ride. I peered through the haze. The elevator walls were decorated with spray paint and magic marker.

I watched them sink to the hallway floor, then said, "When you feel that you can stand, we'll take a walk to the Dean's office. When you guys get better, you'll have a lot of cleaning up to do."

One kid managed to stop choking long enough to say, "What? It wasn't *us*! We didn't do it!"

"Right," I answered. "Of course you did it. This is an open and shut case."

Jokes And Jokers

♦

I have never appreciated practical jokes and developed a distaste for them at an early age. I hated that awful feeling when you're the kid who's getting the ball thrown over your head, making it impossible to get in the game. You know that feeling—and don't you just hate it?

When I was in the second grade, I played a practical joke and pulled a chair out from under the most beautiful girl in class, my first true love, Gwendolyn Tempth. She fell on the floor and hit her head on the back of the seat. She was hurt and crying and looked back at me with tears in her soft brown eyes. She couldn't believe I had done this to her. Although I apologized, Miss Berry, our teacher, was angry. I can still feel Gwendolyn's eyes on me today and can still hear Miss Berry's words, "Sorry doesn't help."

From that day, I have seldom engaged in practical jokes, resorting to them *only* when they were justified—or simply irresistible.

So, I could not help myself when I found the toilet in a South Chicago Heights alley.

It looked as if someone had cleaned it up just before it was removed; kind of the same idea as someone cleaning their house before the cleaning lady comes over or brushing their teeth carefully before going to the dentist to have them extracted. As I drove by the toilet, it cried out to me, "Pick me, pick me." I stopped, put it in the back of my truck and drove back to the high school.

I knew who needed that toilet.

A fellow teacher, Gerald Lauritsen, had been promoted to a Division Coordinator. He was now my immediate supervisor

I needed to play a practical joke on him, something to properly celebrate his new title.

I took away his new high-backed, imitation-leather desk chair and slipped the toilet under his desk. In the morning, he sat down on his new throne and discovered the trick. He was really good natured about the prank but came directly to me and asked for his chair back. He seemed to know who had his property and probably remembered, when he was a step lower on the career ladder and still in the classroom, that I was the one who had stolen his entire class.

You see, Lauritsen, as a teacher, was often on the phone in the office adjoining his classroom and would sometimes forget about the students waiting for him next door. On one occasion I quietly took 28 kids right from under his nose and placed them in the next empty classroom. They huddled in a corner with the lights off. Lauritsen stepped into the dark room, managed to miss seeing the class hiding there, and kept looking for them during the entire class period.

I had instantly reduced his class load. You think he could have thanked me.

But people are like that. After all, Dave Sheridan did not thank me when I presented him with his door at an awards banquet. Dave, a counselor, always talked about his "Open door policy," so I felt I should remind him of it. He left the restaurant with his door sticking out of the trunk of his car. A symbolic gift, I thought, but I'm afraid not properly appreciated.

There were times when I stayed at school after everyone had gone home so I could slip some prize piece of junk into the main office. The principal usually called me to take the thing away. Five consecutive principals have made such calls to me. Each of them must have passed the word along to his successor about whom to call if junk appeared in the main office. The calls followed a familiar pattern:

"Anderson, come and get that old bicycle out of the office lobby."

"Anderson, get over here and remove the spare tire and wheel off the sign-in counter."

"Anderson, remove the bathroom sink you left in here last night."

"Anderson, come and get that welded up metal thing you call a sculpture out of here. We can't lift it…"

One afternoon, I drove a fork lift truck through the hallway to the office, stuck the forks through the doorway and told the secretaries I had come to pick up my check.

Music plays before each tardy bell, usually classical music designed to sooth restless American youth. I sometimes took the Vivaldi or Mozart out and substituted some "Fred Guitar Music" I had written and recorded. I listened with pride before each class period and announced to all who are near, "That's my stuff."

And again the phone call, "Anderson, come and get your tape."

I came in early one morning and started to sign everyone in but was stopped before I really got going. I incurred the wrath of one switch board operator whose job was stuffing all the mailboxes with "pertinent" bulletins and important information. (Have you ever noticed the *bull* in the word *bulletin?*) She twice caught me distributing all my papers in other people's mailboxes. She had no sense of humor and so, under her watchful eye, I abandoned the practice.

Sometimes teachers left a car running outside the building, *running* and *unlocked*, as they went in to the office to sign in. Fifteen hundred kids would be entering the school at the same time. Hard to believe, but some of them were trying to figure out a way to get out of there and were seeking transportation. It did not make much sense to me to leave an unattended car running and I drove more than a few of them away and parked them far out in the parking lot, leaving their owners out hunting them down. No one ever thanked me for keeping their cars safe or preventing a good kid from going bad with an act of car theft.

I never considered these things serious practical jokes. I never really tried to seriously nail anyone with a trick...

Almost never.

Well, only once or twice.

And only when someone really, really, *really* had it coming.

Consider Bill and Bob, two gifted and talented practical jokers. Their last names are not important, nor is the possible law suit for what I might say about them. Besides, they were thought of as a team: Laurel and Hardy. Abbott and Costello. Bill and Bob.

Ah, yes, Bill and Bob. They really had it coming. Really, really.

Bill and Bob team-taught social studies. Working together on curriculum they did some truly innovative things for kids, but working along other lines, they pulled off some amazing jokes. They had generous natures, spreading their jolly jesting around for nearly everyone on the faculty.

But Bill and Bob did focus on one poor teacher in particular, Tom Peterson. The team procured a picture of poor Tom, enlarged it, duplicated it and hung it throughout the building with the caption, THIS MAN NEEDS A DATE. CALL 758-XXXX.

I felt they were unfair. I went around the building and took down the signs.

When the teachers came back from summer vacation, our faculty association asked us to respond to a questionnaire, "What did you do over the summer break?"

Bill and Bob filled out and submitted the form for their victim of choice. They explained that Tom had had a fine summer working as a bouncer at the Isle of Capri, a local gay bar featuring transvestites, cross dressers, and female impersonators and submitted it in his name.

The faculty newsletter carried this newsy item.

I went to see Bill and Bob. I appealed to their sense of fair play. I was under the illusion that I could exert some tempering influence on their persecution of this man. I asked could they refine their humor with, perhaps, a little compassion.

Bob explained to me, "Oh, he loves it, Fred. Trust me. He revels in the attention."

Bill said, "He has a sign on him that says, KICK ME. Maybe you can't see it, but it's there. He wears it all the time."

One day, poor Tom walked out of the school, head down, looking like the world would come to an end within the next 30 seconds.

"What's wrong?" I asked.

"Those guys," he responded, "they glued my paper weight to my desk."

"Let me go upstairs with you and see if I can get it loose." I responded.

"Don't bother," he said. "I broke it loose, but it tore off a big section of my desk."

"Come on," I said. "Let's go get them. I've got a hydraulic jack in the shop. We'll lift up their cars and set them both up on cement blocks with the wheels off the ground. We can do it in a half hour."

"No," he said. "Let it go. I just want to go home." I'd been walking alongside him and hadn't seen what he held in the hand that he now raised and stared at: the paper weight still attached to a Masonite piece of the desk top. I think there was a tear in his eye. I could see the *KICK ME* sign for the first time.

More?

Certainly.

One day, Bill and Bob fired Tom. They took a piece of Superintendent Barnhardt's stationery and wrote Tom that the school was proud of the fine work he had done while he had been there, but his department was being downsized, and, though regretfully, the district would have to let him go.

Tom smelled a rat and immediately went to Bill and Bob. "You guys," he said with a smile, letting them know he was in on the joke.

The team snatched away the letter and read it as if for the first time. They appeared distraught, concerned, and upset that their good friend was on the way out.

"We'll go to bat for you," they said. "We'll save your job." They sent around petitions and solicited signatures to save his position. At this point he was thoroughly convinced that he *was* losing his job and it was not until he saw next year's contract that he became convinced that he would be rehired.

Finally, the practical joking tag team went too far. They told Tom someone was drowning in the swimming pool. Out of concern for human life and having skills as a certified paramedic, Tom raced down a flight of stairs, through the building and to the rescue only to find the joke was once again on him.

It had to happen and was perhaps overdue: the administration had a serious talk with Bill and Bob.

The jokes on Tom Peterson stopped.

The Bill and Bob pranks on others, however, did not.

The team ran the TV broadcasting program and needed a boom to hold a microphone during interviews. One of our students, David, had terrific woodworking ability and offered to build the unit in his father's workshop. He constructed the boom from walnut. It rode on three large wheels and the microphone arm could be extended at least six feet and was counter weighted with an open box in which stones could be added for balance. It was a prize, a beautiful piece of work, but the team kept putting off paying him for his materials. They finally wrote a check against a small account they had established for their activity. They wrote the check for $3,000 and then wrote void across it. The team thought it was a great joke, but the kid came to see me.

He showed me the check. He was really upset. "This isn't fair, Mr. Anderson," he said. "They promised to pay me for my work but look: Void! I'll *never* get paid."

"Let me call your mom," I said. "I think we can show these guys they made a big mistake and we can get you paid."

I had met David's mother at an open house. She was a sharp woman with a commendable sense of justice—and humor. Yes, she would definitely help.

The next day David was strategically missing from the team's class. Marie Robertson, a member of the same department, came to talk to the team. She told them she heard David was in some kind of trouble. Something had happened in the community. Did they know anything about it?

They said no.

David's mother called the team on their office phone. She needed to talk with David. He wasn't in class? Why, she knew he had left that morning to go to school. Where could he be, what was going on? Bill and Bob did not know.

Enter police officer, Jerry Sill, who shows up at the Bill and Bob classroom door.

He had the $3,000 check in his hand. He asked if they had written the check? The word *VOID* was whited out. David had been picked up in town with a large amount of cash in his possession. David had cashed the check and the police wanted to know why they had given a 15 year old boy so much money.

"Oh, no!" cried Bill.

"Oh, no!" cried Bob.

"There's only 50 dollars in that account!" cried Bill and Bob.

Bill and Bob worried all day long. I waited for them to go home and as they were leaving I went up to them and said, "It's a joke, guys. It's all a joke."

"I knew it was a joke," said Bob.

"Sure," I said, "sure you did."

And so, I had paid them back. I'd zinged them good—for Tom Peterson, for David, and for the rest of us who had been victimized. It felt good.

But...

Deep, deep inside, I had this feeling: it was not over. It would never be over. *Vendetta!*

They would come for me: Payback!

I would have to wait.

And so, I wait and wait and wait.

I'm still waiting.

Jesse James had A Plate in His Head

◆ _____

"Where's your hall pass?" I asked the kid dressed in his P.E. uniform. "You're a mile away from the gym."

"I don't have a pass," he answered. "Mr. Versypt threw me out of class. I'm goin' to the dean."

"He must have been really mad to send you out without a pass," I said. "What did you do?"

"I went over to the girls' side of the gym, and took down my shorts."

I studied the boy for a moment, then asked, "What did the girls do?"

"I'm pretty big," he stated with a smirk. "Some of them wanted a second look."

"I'll walk you to the dean," I told him. "What's your name?"

"Jesse James," he answered, "I'm Jesse James."

With a little luck, that would have been the last of him, but the next semester I found Jesse in my woodshop class.

Jesse would not pay attention. He was disruptive and talked out of turn. He picked on other students, and when he worked on machines, he was scary.

I talked to his counselor, Del Mach. "Del," I said, "the kids's a problem."

"I know," Del said, "he has a plate in his head. You'll have to make allowances. His mother said when he was a baby, he played in the alley and was run over by a garbage truck."

"He has a plate in his head?"

"The doctors put a plate in his head to cover his brain. His mom said from that point on his behavior was erratic. No, she didn't say erratic. She said that from that point on he was goofy."

"Del," I asked, "don't you think it was kind of goofy to name the kid Jesse?"

"I think it was goofy to let the kid play in the alley," Del said.

I tried to make allowances for Jesse and so did the rest of the staff. But sometimes he was too much. I had to watch him constantly: he threw things.

The woodshop class and I built a Santa Claus house. We designed the structure to fit on a large trailer, and when it was finished it was moved downtown. The Chicago Heights Chamber of Commerce needed the portable unit for a white Santa on Mondays, Wednesdays, and Fridays, and a black Santa on Tuesdays, Thursdays, and Saturdays. The Santa Claus house was supposed to help the (now defunct) Chicago Heights downtown area. The new malls were giving the older stores a serious challenge, more serious than they could handle. The town decided a rainbow of Santas might help the merchants' Christmas season and spread a little racial good will at the same time.

The class built the walls in our shop, then moved them to the trailer. I taught them how to fit the windows and set the rafters on the building as it sat on its wheels in the faculty parking lot.

The 16 penny nails started to disappear faster than we were using them, and the faculty began to discover the nails, one by one, in their tires. Jesse James had a great pitching arm and could throw a 16 penny nail harder and farther than anyone I had ever known. When the faculty complained, I told them, "I'm doing the best I can, but Jesse James is throwing the nails. You'll have to make some allowances. Remember folks, Jesse James has a plate in his head."

I found Jesse in the halls again without a pass. He was dressed in his P.E. uniform, and when he walked closer, I could see the armpit of his shirt was blood soaked. "What happened, Jesse? Are you hurt? Can I help you?"

"I was trying to do an 'Iron Cross' on the rings," he told me. "I got shot in the arm last night with a 22 and I tore open my wound. I'm goin' to the nurse."

"I'll walk along with you," I said.

It was the last time I would walk along with Jesse.

Jesse never graduated. Before he turned 18, someone shot him again. They buried Jesse James with a plate in his head.

An Eye for An Eye

———————— ◆ ————————

I weaved in and out of the hallway traffic trying to get a look at the kids' jean jackets. The art work caught my attention and there was some lettering I couldn't read. The jackets disappeared into the river of kids hustling to class leaving me with one fleeting glimpse: A big eye crudely drawn on one and more eyes staring back at me from the other. There must be a new gang in town, I thought and promised myself I'd get a better look the next morning.

But I didn't see the kids and didn't have the chance to read the words that accompanied the eyes until the semester changed. Then I found the two kids in my new class, sitting next to each other at a back workbench. I called the class roll and now the two kids had names. As I lectured I moved around the room and slipped behind them where I could see their jackets. Bill Sanders's jacket with the one big eye said, *No Eye*, and Bob Miller's jacket carried three big eyes in a triangle and said, *Three Eyes*.

When the kids turned in their written work, I found the symbols and nicknames on their papers. "Why do you call yourself *No Eye*?" I asked Bill Sanders.

Bill held one of his eyes wide open and tapped the pupil with his pencil. *Thunk, thunk, thunk...* "False," he said. "I have no eye."

"Ask Bob why they call him *Three Eyes*," one of my new students said.

"All right," I answered, turning to Bob. "Why do they call you *Three Eyes*?"

"We'll have to show you," said Bob. "You'll have to see the whole thing. It's something we've done every since grammar school, ever since I put Bill's eye out with a BB gun. Stand out in the hall tomorrow, Mr. Anderson. Wait for us to come to class and we will show you the whole effect."

"It's really neat, Mr. Anderson," the class spokesman said. "You have *got* to see it. It's really neat."

And so the next morning, before their class met, I waited in the hall until Bob, *One Eye* and his best friend, Bill, *Three Eyes*, walked toward me. They had their inside arms around each other's necks, their heads touched at the temples. Bill's free hand opened wide his empty eye socket; you could look right inside his head. Bob held both his eyes wide open and held Bill's eye in his mouth. They were humming as they walked towards me, humming in a low monotone.

"Isn't it neat?" asked the class spokesman. "They do it all the time. Isn't it neat?"

"Gross," said one of the girls waiting for class.

"Hummmmm," went *No Eye* and *Three Eyes*.

Messin' With My Bird

◆

I didn't think the guinea hen and I had to worry about Helen Norton. Helen may have been the first to notice the inter-species breeding in the school's courtyard, and may have asked me just what I was trying to prove with those rabbits and the hen, but she was too busy as the English Department Chairman to be "messin'" with my bird.

The hen had come from nowhere. She must have caught a good wind, become airborne, and flown over the building into the courtyard where I raised the rabbits. I brought her some poultry grain. Soon after that, Denny, the large blue buck rabbit, bred her a few times and she began to lay eggs in the little house I built for her.

A week later, a student announced, "Mr. Anderson! Mrs. Norton is in the courtyard, messin' with your guinea hen!"

"Everything is probably all right," I told the kid.

"No!" he returned. "She was doin' somethin' in the hen's box. I thought that was your bird."

"Don't worry about Mrs. Norton," I said to him. "She is probably checking to see the hen has food and water."

"The food and water is on the *outside* of the box. Mrs. Norton was right *inside* the nest box. I think she's stealin' your eggs!"

Later that day I unlocked the courtyard door to check the food and water and gather my eggs. Quite a crowd watching today, I thought as I looked through the glass into the hallway. Looks like the whole English Department is down on the first floor.

I reached in and grabbed the first egg. "This egg is fuzzy and blue," I said silently to myself, "and so are the rest of them." I took the eggs out, one by one.

"Can we see your fuzzy blue eggs, Fred?" one of the English teachers called as the group chuckled along with Helen.

"May I see your fuzzy eggs is proper English," I reminded the group. "And yes, you may see my fuzzy eggs, but actually they are Helen's. Good joke, Helen."

"I didn't flock those eggs, Fred," she replied. "They are the results of the rabbit breeding the hen, and nothing more," she said laughing.

"Then you'd better contact the newspaper, Helen," I told her. "When these eggs hatch, there's gonna be a lot of hoppin' and flappin' goin' on. This science experiment could put us on the map."

Blood on the Wall

◆

The wire-mesh safety glass was smashed, and there was blood on the metal door frame. Blood was splashed on the wall, and pooled on the floor. I followed the red trail into the metal shop, where I found Andre Rhymes, kneeling before the long stainless steel sink. His arms were drooped over the rim, his head hung in the bowl. The swirling water was streaked red; Andre was bleeding to death.

Several deep gashes ran across his right forearm, several more across his left. He moaned, fought to get his feet under him, then sunk back to his knees.

If I go to a telephone, I thought, this kid is going to die. "Andre," I said to him, "I'm going to get you out of here and down to the nurse." I grabbed the arm closest to me, ducked down, then wiggled between the kid and the sink. Before he slid from my back, I clamped his two leaky arms with my fingers, then pulled him toward me. Thank God this kid weighs under 110 pounds, I thought, as I transferred his weight across my shoulders, and then struggled to rise.

I carried Andre out of the metal shop and passed the broken hallway door. He must have been running, stiff-armed the door—and missed the frame.

Richard Nolan walked out of the little theater, where his English class had been watching a film. "Rich," I called, "I need some help clamping this kid together."

"What the hell happened here?" Rich asked. He swung into position and applied pressure to a few places I could not reach. Together we carried Andre to the nurse.

"This kid is a mess," an ambulance worker said, as they carried Andre out the door, "but I think you may have caught this in time. Does anyone know his blood type?"

Rich and I cleaned up after the ambulance had gone. "Do you know that Andre is probably the meanest kid in school?" Rich asked me.

"I know," I said.

"There will be some people who will say we should have let him bleed to death."

"Maybe some of the meanness leaked out of him today."

"He leaked all over us," Rich said, looking at his shirt and trousers.

After several weeks, Andre returned to school. "It took 27 stitches," he proudly told me, showing me his forearms, "to close me up. And I was two pints low. That's almost a quart. They had to give me blood."

"I'm glad to see you, Andre," I said. "How are you feeling?"

"I feel better," he said. "My mom said to find you and tell you thanks. So...so thanks."

"Anything else?"

"Nope," he said. "That's it."

Is That You, Mr. Anderson?

◆

The young woman waded towards me and wrinkled up her face. "Mr. Anderson," she asked quizzically, "is that *you*?"

I stared at her briefly, all of her, and she was staring at me. The water was shallow. There was no place to hide.

"Mr. Anderson," she repeated, squinting, "is that really you? I didn't recognize you without my glasses."

"Harriet," I replied, "I didn't recognize you without your clothes."

At school there is an invisible barrier between the students on one side of my teacher's desk and me on the other. Our personal and private lives are separated from each other. But here was Harriet, a student from my home room. She and her friends had driven an old Volkswagen bus to our secluded gravel pit swimming hole. They shed their clothing and ran into the water before Joan, our children and I could scramble for cover.

In one brief moment Harriet and I were on common ground, standing there in the water, and things would never be the same; we had seen each other in the nude.

The Broken Building

◆

I arrived at the first teachers' meeting at the beginning of the school year, and looked in disbelief at the new addition. Trucks and equipment blocked the entrance, stacks of material still lay in the parking lot, and pieces of stone and large clumps of clay littered the sidewalks. Our Freshman/Sophomore school had been upgraded over the summer to become the four-year Bloom Trail High School. The building was supposed to be ready for students in three days, but it sure didn't look as if the workmen would meet the deadline.

Inside, things were not as bad; they were worse. The hall ways were cluttered with pallets stacked with floor tile. Five gallon buckets of mastic lined one wall and hunks of steel studding lay everywhere. There were areas throughout the new section where the ceiling and floor tiles were yet to be installed. Walls remained unpainted, and lights in some rooms, non-operational.

I was not the only teacher who arrived early to check out the new facilities. Consensus of opinion, shared by the munching donuts and sipping coffee group, was that we were not ready to open; the new school year would not start on time. Nope. No way. It did not make sense.

The first administrator began the morning meeting. "Don't be too disturbed," he said, "if you feel your classrooms need a little polish. We realize that some rooms, although close to completion, are, as of today, not *quite* ready. We have been assured, by the general contractor, that

58

everything will *indeed* be ready for our students by the day after tomorrow. The general contractor has *emphasized* that the tradesmen, working in and outside the building, will work long hours to ready our facilities prior to the arrival of students. He tells me, he and his crew are *committed* to the educational philosophies of this district and…"

The man was going on and on, but then made the mistake of recognizing a few of us who had raised our hands.

"I don't think this place is ready to see students," one teacher called to him. "The lights in my classroom don't work." There was a murmuring throughout the room.

"No lights? *How about no floor!*" cried out another. "There are no tiles on the cement floor, and I haven't been able to find a ceiling in there, or lights to even turn on."

"I checked out the new swimming pool, and there are two-by-fours and a construction ladder floating around in the water," a PE teacher announced.

I knew that. I had wanted to be the first kid in the pool, so I went in early the morning before, pushed that construction ladder to one side and jumped in the cold water. "Geez, that water was cold. I almost froze my…"

"Now just a minute!" our administrator, our *leader*, said, bringing my mind back to the meeting. "Your concerns will be addressed *in time*. We will all have to learn to improvise to a small degree, and have some patience. We have worked hard this summer to bring you and our students the very finest, four-year comprehensive high school. I have told you…I have told you…told you, I have *emphasized*…that things will be ready, that some of us will continue to work these long, long hours to…"

When he finished, he turned the meeting over to the second administrator, then quickly made for the door.

"Greetings to you all," the new speaker began, "and welcome back. I trust that you had a restful summer. I couldn't help but notice you had a few concerns."

"I went into the men's room and couldn't find any toilet paper," one teacher called out.

"I went into the girl's washroom," called out another, "and I could not find a toilet. Just a lot of holes in the floor where the toilets are *supposed* to go…"

The second administrator quickly turned the meeting over to the newly hired *third* administrator, who welcomed us all back as if there were no problems. No, no problems.

Take a matter such as attendance. There were no problems with the attendance policy; our school *had* no written attendance policy.

"What? No attendance policy?" challenged one teacher. "With our kids, we won't survive without an attendance policy!"

"Now listen here!" bellowed Administrator Number Three, "I'm new here, and so is your new school. New! We're both new, and deserve that chance that I know you will give us. We feel instead of copying existing school attendance policies, we should invent our own, so to speak, as we go along. We will provide for these young people…"

He tried to finish up, but we just wouldn't let him. He would have turned the meeting over to someone else, but there was no Fourth Administrator, nor Designated Scapegoat. They had all escaped, leaving him to face our questions—and our anger, building by the minute.

He made for the door, leaving us to mumble among ourselves and wonder just who was in charge.

But the place is unsafe, I thought. *That's the bottom line. We are in for a bumpy ride. This is going to be quite a year.*

And, so…

It should have been a wonderful time. It should have been our greatest hour. But from the moment students arrived, to the morning we locked the angry mob outside the building, things went wrong, wronger, and wrong to the ultimate.

Some of the student class schedules weren't ready the first day; we called back buses and sent a batch of kids home.

Rooms had been renumbered during the summer; students who had schedules wandered in search of classrooms. When they found the rooms, some were overcrowded and there were no places to sit down. One study hall in the cafeteria held three hundred and fifty students with only a single teacher to supervise them.

Areas under construction were unsecured. After several days, some students discovered these "unsecured areas," and used them to hide. They found the unlocked tunnel system and traveled unimpeded under the building.

Students came to school late. They took multiple lunch periods. They drove to school, then left early. Students at Bloom Trail High School enjoyed their freedom—they enjoyed far too much freedom.

These kids came from three different towns. Some of them were racially mixed together for the first time. Black students and White students gathered in Black groups and White groups, then roamed the hallways before school. They wandered around the outside campus during lunchtime and throughout the parking lots at the end of the school day. Establishing their territory and setting the boundaries, both groups were noisy, and rowdy, sometimes shouting racial insults at each other. Rumors were common, and students wandered about, looking for the next verbal confrontation.

The "confusion" continued throughout that first week, and day by day, student behavior became worse. An assistant principal, in an attempt to control a new rumor, grabbed the microphone and made this classic announcement over the intercom: "Contrary to the rumors, there is *not* going to be a riot in the cafeteria during sixth hour."

"What the hell did he just say?" a teacher sitting next to me at the lunch table cried. "I don't believe he just said that!"

Kids poured from rooms throughout the building and into the comparatively calm lunchroom.

Then all hell broke loose.

It was September 14. That was the day we lost control. Black and White groups of students roamed the first and second floor. At first, some of us who had been assigned to keep order faced them, but we were swallowed up in the crowds. The groups walked, ran, then sprinted down the hallways in search of each other. They refused to go to class and finally emptied outside the building and into the parking lot.

Fighting erupted outside the building. A group of Black kids retreated to the safety of the building and pulled the crash bars closed. Together we held back the outside mob.

I could hear the yelling through the closed door, then the sound of rubble hitting the building and the glass entrance doors.

"Get away from the glass," I shouted to the kids inside, and for the first time that morning, I felt that someone was listening to me. The Black kids moved away from the doorway and toward the center of the building. I was alone at the door, watching the White mob outside.

I heard the sound of broken glass in the stairwell on the second floor. Small rocks continued to pepper the door's glass, and then I saw the kid run toward my door and heave the boulder.

I turned my head as the rock came through, carrying the plate glass to the hallway floor. The mob sounded louder through the opening, and inside, I heard glass being knocked out throughout the west side.

They were destroying the new building! I thought. They were wrecking the place! There would be nothing left and there was absolutely no way to stop it!

Up to this point, I had been too angry to be scared, but now I wondered if we'd all get out alive. It took over an hour for the police to arrive, to clear the building, and for us to organize the buses to take the kids home. The police arrested 17 students. We later suspended 50; some were expelled and never came back.

We closed the doors until September 20th, then tried again with an abbreviated schedule. Periods were shortened, lunch periods eliminated, and activities postponed. Students were not allowed to drive and "Open Campus" was discontinued. There was an emphasis on rumor control and parents helped patrol the halls.

Our new school had a reputation that would stay with us for years.

Today, when students ask why they don't have an "open campus" and why they can't go out for lunch, when they ask why the attendance policy is so strict, I tell them, "Ask your mothers and fathers. Some of them should remember the day the kids broke the building."

Jim Krygier And the Vampire Stakes

◆

Jim Krygier, the PE Department Chairman, walked into my second hour woodworking class. "Fred," he called over the drone of the shop machinery, "do you have a minute?"

I shut down the bandsaw I was using. "Sure, Jim, what's on your mind?"

"Can you make a couple of three or four foot sticks out of some scrap pieces laying around, and put a sharp point on them?"

"How about those two pieces standing in the corner, Jim? I can point them on the disk sander. Going after vampires?" I asked. "It's too cold for tomato stakes. I hope you're not planting your garden."

"You might be interested in this," he said. "I am going hunting, and you have your conference period next hour. Interested in going along? Meet me down in PE immediately after this class."

I found Jim in front of the boys' locker room, five minutes after third hour began. I held his pointed sticks to the side as the class, in gym uniforms, rushed through the open doors and passed us in the hallway.

One of the PE teachers called from inside the locker room, "Everybody out? I'm lockin' up! Everybody out?" He hung back a minute, after his class had gone, then emerged and locked the locker room door. "What you doing, Jim?" he asked, looking at the pointed sticks.

"We're going hunting," Jim whispered to him.

"We got rats? Vampires?" the guy asked.

Jim whispered, "Yeah, we got rats *and* vampires. I'll talk to you later." The teacher looked at us quizzically, then hurried to join his class.

Jim put his finger to his lips. "Shhh." He slipped the key in the lock and turned the bolt. Slowly opening the squeaking door with one hand, he reached for a pointed stick with the other, then motioned me to follow him into the darkened musty-smelling room.

We tiptoed along the block wall passageway, past the dimly-lit discarded sweat socks, towels, and a jock strap on the floor. What was the guy doing?

Jim moved toward an old wooden chest. He pointed his stick down into the opening and motioned for me to do the same at the chest in the far corner. "Poke away!" he called.

Ah, what the hell, I thought, jabbing through the towels. If it'll make him happy...

"*Hey*! Stop that!" a muffled voice screamed from my bin. "Cut it out! Stop it, you sonofabitch!" I jumped back as the towels parted and a form arose, draped in blue-green terrycloth.

"Empty your pockets," I heard Jim order a second figure, standing in his bin. "Fred, take that towel off his head, and have him empty his pockets!"

"You heard Mr. Krygier," I demanded of the boy standing in front of me. "Empty your pockets."

"You had no right to poke me!" the kid shouted at the pointed stick, but he emptied his pockets. "You go around *poking* people..."

"Put the stuff on the bench," I said, looking at the money, watches, and rings he held. *I* was not *nice*. I went around *poking* people.

"We've been after you kids for a long time. This is the stuff you took yesterday," Jim said, scooping up the valuables stolen the day before from the gym class. "I couldn't figure out how you got into this locked room day after day. You were in here all the time, weren't you?"

"It wasn't us," one kid whined.

"What if we give it back?" the other asked.

"You shouldn't have poked us with the sticks," said the first.

Jim looked at me and laughed. "Glad you came along, Fred?" he asked. "New experience. After all, you've never gone vampire hunting with me before."

Robin Chapman Changes Her Name to Prudence

◆

I asked Robin Chapman, who teaches English, if I could tell her story. She said that I could, but only if I changed her name to Prudence.

When the "incident" in Prudence's classroom occurred word got around quickly. The students all seemed to know (and the faculty found out almost as fast), that a kid sat in the front of her classroom, by her desk. While she was teaching, he masturbated.

It was Prudence's first teaching assignment; she was young, fresh out of college. She told me she had gone out in the hallway, away from him and the class, and cried.

The students whispered about the thing that happened, but the faculty, attempting to make her feel at home in her new school, complimented her for being an inspiring teacher, someone who turned kids on, who fired them up, who brought them around, who made them feel just so *comfortable*. The compliments went on and on; we were all pretty insensitive.

When I asked Prudence if I could use her name, I also asked if she remembered what the kid looked like.

Prudence answered, "He was tall and skinny, Fred, lanky with a pale complexion."

The description fit what I imagined him to be.

"What happened to him? Do you still keep in touch?" I asked, thinking I was real funny.

"His counselor didn't believe me," she answered. "I don't feel the young man got the help he needed. He went on to molest some young girl and was eventually killed in an armed robbery at a convenience store."

"Was he just a poor bystander that got in the way?" I asked.

"No," she answered. "He was robbing the place, and didn't get out before the police arrived."

"Do you suppose he stopped to masturbate?" I asked.

She laughed, and said, "Do you know, Fred, I always wondered about that. Maybe he just pulled out the wrong gun."

I Meet Captain Dynamite

◆

I thought the usual angry/frustrated thoughts you get when the world doesn't do all it could to fit into your plans. A crowd at the 84 Lumber Company? How was I supposed to pick up my load of 2 x 4s with all these people here?

The sign advertised:

CAPTAIN DYNAMITE!
10% OFF ON HAND TOOLS!
FREE HOT DOGS! FREE!

The parking lot was choked with people, fans of hand tools, hot dogs, or dynamite. I needed to get close to load that lumber for my Monday morning's Construction Trades Class.

I parked on the street, then walked toward the building. There had to be a way around this mess.

I was debating crowd infiltration techniques when Captain Dynamite approached me. At least, that's who I assumed he was: he wore a flashy jump suit and carried a goggled helmet decorated with the American flag.

"Hi," he called, extending his hand, "I'm Captain Dynamite. Would you mind moving your truck down the road? I'm going to blow myself up in 15 minutes and your truck is too close." Captain Dynamite gestured toward a trunk size box, color coordinated with his uniform and positioned in the small field between the street and the store.

"Move your truck, okay," he continued. "Then come back and have a hot dog on me. Tell them Captain Dynamite sent you."

My truck looked far enough away to me, I thought. To move it farther would make loading more difficult. Who was this yahoo in the long red underwear giving me parking instructions?

But I went along with the program, moving the truck to a spot three-quarters of a block away, then returned for my free hot dog. "Captain Dynamite sent me," I told the hot dog vender. I was beginning to get in the carnival mood and had forgotten my lumber mission.

"The hot dog is already free," said the vender, motioning to the sign.

Captain Dynamite stepped out on the field. Walking toward the box, he took a microphone and announced, "I'm going to blow myself up. Cover your ears and watch for flying debris. I want *everyone* to be safe."

Captain Dynamite put on his helmet, pulled tight the chin strap, adjusted his goggles, stepped into the box, and with a wave to the crowd pulled down the lid.

I had seen this trick on TV once before. There would be an audible pop, a puff of smoke, the box would fall apart and the stunt man would stagger around a bit. He'd take off his helmet and wave again to the crowd. It would be a great trick, I thought as I chewed on the hot dog, but then the box blew up.

I had not covered my ears.

And the box really *blew up*.

Blowing up—exploding—*loud!*

My hands went toward my ears, but it was too late. Everything rang with the sound of the blast as pieces of the box blew high into the sky and in all directions. One big chunk wafted towards my truck and floated the distance into the back of the pickup's bed.

Dust settled in the field revealing Captain Dynamite kneeling in the space where his box had been. He slowly stood, then wobbled in place. He vibrated, stumbled, then dropped to his knees. Captain Dynamite clutched his helmet, then rolled on his back.

His assistant rushed to help him remove his helmet and gloves. Blood ran from the Captain's nose.

Captain Dynamite reached for the microphone. He paused a moment and then Captain spoke in a small, soft, shaky voice, "It was a really big charge. A *big* charge—big. This is the last time I'll blow myself up."

I left the store with my ears ringing and without my 2 x 4s, but with a piece of Captain Dynamite's final explosion in the back of the pickup.

I had been witness to the end of a show business tradition: Captain Dynamite's Last Blast.

He had (ahem!) retired with a bang.

Continuing Education

———————◆———————

"How old are you, Tom?" Bill McGee, the principal, asked the young man with the guitar case. "You've been around here longer than I have. When are you going to graduate?"

"Maybe next year," Tom Gurney slowly replied, "I think I'll graduate next year."

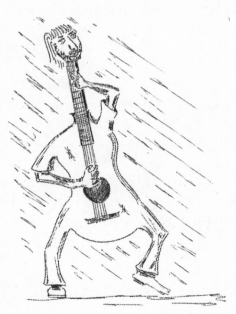

"The records show you've been in high school for six going on seven years," Principal McGee said. "And you're going to be 21 this year? What's taking you so long?"

"High school has always been a good place for me," Tom said. "I behave myself and get along with everyone."

"That's not the problem," the principal said. "It's just that you're getting so old, Tom, soon you'll be older than some of your *teachers*. Do you know how many credits you need to graduate? Do you know how many credits you have?"

"I *think* I'm a sophomore," Tom said. "I'm smart enough to do the work, but playing with my band keeps me out pretty late."

"Let me tell you what we're going to do…I am going to create a number of Independent Study courses for you," Bill McGee said. "We'll find some of your teachers that will go along with this and we'll finally get you out of here."

"Why are you doing this for me?" Tom asked.

"Because you are going to go someplace with your music, Tom. You may not be a great student, but you are a great musician, and I want you to say you graduated from Bloom Trail High School."

And so Tom minstreled his way through his last year of high school, writing songs about science, singing old folk ballads in his English class, polishing his guitar in woodshop, and taking solos in music. The principal gave "independent study status" to these activities and Tom walked down the aisle at graduation, just before his 21st birthday, with his classmates (if not exactly his peer group).

Jim's Car

◆

"Why is your Mercedes running in the parking lot?" I asked Jim Atherton, our business teacher.

"It's a diesel," he answered. "I have trouble starting it in the winter. When I talked to my German mechanic, he asked, 'You shut it off? It's a diesel Mercedes Benz, and it's winter. Let it run, Mr. Atherton. Let it run.'"

"How long are you going to keep this up, Jim?" I asked.

"I don't know exactly," Jim replied, "but you know, Fred, it's the end of February, and it's almost spring."

"Aren't you worried that someone might steal it?" I asked.

"It's locked up," he said, "and someone would have to break inside."

I had the feeling that if someone would have stolen the car, Jim would have gladly waved it good-by.

Unstealing the Bicycle

◆

Anthony Santori was late to class again. He looked as if he had been sleeping in his clothes. Anthony needed to wash up and as I got closer to him I smelled liquor on his breath.

"What's going on, Anthony?" I asked him. "You're an hour late to class, and it looks as if you've been out all night…"

"I missed the bus and had to find another way to get to school," he answered.

"Let's go out in the hall and talk."

Anthony followed me through the classroom door. "Did you ride your bike here?" I asked, looking at the girls' model green bike, leaning against the hallway wall.

"Yeah, I rode it here. It's got a broken kick stand," he said, glancing at the bike balanced against the wall.

"Why don't you go in the washroom and clean up, Anthony. I don't want you to work today." I was concerned: he was probably still a little drunk. "Can I get you something to eat?" I asked.

"Just coffee, Mr. Anderson. My stomach is messed up, but I really *need* a cup of coffee."

After the two hour work session was over, Anthony left with his classmates and walked towards the bus.

"Hey, Anthony," I called. "What about your bike? Are you going to leave it here?"

"Yeah," he said, "I don't need it anymore. You can have it if you want it."

"Wait a minute, Anthony. Come back here. Don't get on that bus!"

"Come on, Mr. Anderson," Anthony whined. "I just *borrowed* the bike and I'm through with it. Besides, I don't feel well. I want to go home."

"Who did you borrow the bike from?" I asked.

"From someone's backyard."

"Whose backyard?"

"Someone who lives on Wallace."

"I'll take you home," I said. "You *and* the bike. We'll put it in my pickup and return it to the right backyard."

"Geez!" Anthony cried. "It's no big deal! It's only a bike."

Anthony rode with me in the pickup. We discussed issues of "right and wrong." I sensed he wasn't fascinated by ethical concepts; perhaps it required too much thought for someone with a hangover.

I could tell he was glad when we got to Wallace Street. He jumped out of the cab, got in the pickup's bed and rode along with the bike down the alley looking for the correct yard. He rapped on the cab top and I stopped. Anthony jumped out of the truck, hoisted the bike out and over the fence, and it was done!

He had unstolen the bicycle.

I didn't feel like Father Flanagan at Boy's Town—but close.

Anthony got back in the truck and as I drove him home, I asked, "Are you sure that was the right backyard?"

"Yeah. That was the place. It looked like the place. I think it was the place." He thought for a moment. "Yeah, it was the place."

I happened to tell the story of unstealing the bicycle 20 years later to a former student, Martin Utermark.

"You know, I lived over on Wallace," Martin said. "Someone took my sister's bike out of the backyard while we were at school."

"What color was the bike?" I asked. "Did it have a broken kickstand and did you ever get it back?"

"The kickstand *was* broken and it was a girls' green racing bike. No, never got it back."

"Sorry, Martin," I said to him. "I tried."

The Hit or Miss

◆

Who knows how long the old engine sat in the middle of the corn crib on the abandoned farm, or who pushed her under the leaky roof to protect her from the weather? I do know that each time I visited the old place, to poke around, looking for old glass bottles, pieces of harness, or rusty tools, I'd peek in the corn crib and there she'd be.

I began to think about the machine, the *Hit or Miss,* throughout the week. I thought about her big smooth flywheel, what work she might have done on the farm, and the sound she'd make if she were running. I had heard engines like this at Antique Power Shows and marveled how they idled along forever on a teaspoon's worth of gas. "Bang bang," they'd fire or hit. "*Fitt fitt fitt fitt fitt,*" they'd coast or miss. "*Bang bang, Fitt fitt fitt fitt fitt.*" I loved to hear them run. I loved the pattern of the sound: the hit and miss.

I wondered who owned the Hit or Miss, if he'd be willing to sell her, and then I'd dismiss the idea as foolish. After all, she was in poor repair. On one visit, I discovered she had no compression. I had turned her big flywheel over and there was no resistance.

On another visit I noticed her cylinder head had been cracked, then welded; the job had not been done at all well. Part of her magneto was missing. Her spark plug was broken off clean.

And besides, she was big, just *too* big. I'd kill myself trying to move her, and, really, I had no place to keep her; the garage was full.

Still I found myself returning to the old farm on my way home from work. Not often, really, seldom more than once a week. There she'd be, in the crib, standing in the dirt, in the mud, if it had been raining…

She was waiting, just waiting.

Well, hadn't the farm been abandoned? The engine was just sitting there, an abandoned engine on an abandoned farm…

I began thinking of her as mine. The owner was probably long gone, but just before I took her away, something changed.

The old farmhouse, with broken windows and missing front door, had new windows and a new door fitted. The door was closed now, secured with a pad lock threaded through a hasp bolted to the outside. I peered through a new window. A circular saw stood on the kitchen floor. Drywall had been stacked against one wall and I could see someone had started to install insulation batting between the old studs of an exterior wall. Someone had taken on the property; the abandoned farm and the abandoned engine were not abandoned.

The Hit or Miss was no longer fair game.

But I thought about her; I thought about her. I was thinking about the Hit or Miss on the day I broke Mandy the pony to cart. If I had my mind on breaking Mandy the pony to cart, where it belonged, I might have promptly, even agilely, bailed out when Mandy flipped the damn cart over. Instead I hung on through the upside-down ride, the rough landing, and the grinding slide.

I distinctly heard the snap of the cart's shafts and the snap of my breaking foot, and the pain took my mind away from the Hit or Miss.

The day after my hospital visit, on the way to pick up a load of hay for Mandy, I visited the Hit or Miss one more time. No one was working at the farm house and so I swung my cast out of the pick-up's cab and crutched over to where I found her, still waiting in the corn crib.

But this time she was not quite alone. She was piled up with junk and surrounded by pieces of discarded metal from old cars and farm

equipment. What a shame, I thought. The Hit or Miss is surely abandoned now. Abandoned and cast aside with the rest of this junk.

I paused to ponder the fate of abandoned engines and junk. I could
not be savior to the Hit or Miss. Without the means to pull her free, then
hoist her into the pick-up, I could not rescue her from the junk yard.

I left the farm.

I left the Hit or Miss behind.

The engine was still in my mind when I pulled in my driveway with
the load of hay. I was tired and although the farmer had helped by
throwing the bales down from his loft into the truck, I had stacked them
myself. My cast and crutches slowed the job down, and after a short rest
in the house, I would have to load the hay up in my own loft.

I was still thinking about the Hit or Miss when I crutched back to the
truck loaded with hay. I was pondering issues of right and wrong, fine
points of ownership of the Hit or Miss, questions of borrowing, claim-
ing, taking possession or stealing, as I backed up.

I was not considering ethics or engines when I heard the crunching
sound. In fact, I felt that crunch through the tailgate, through those hay
bales, through the back of my neck and right on down into the broken
bone plastered up inside my cast.

Why, that was the station wagon behind me, our *new* station wagon,
our personal possession, right of ownership station wagon. I considered
this: *I have crunched our new car. I have wrecked my very own thing!*

I clung to the small hope that all was not lost. I sat still for a moment;
I hadn't the strength to move. There was no blood in my head. Some
phenomenon of circulation was sending it down into my broken foot.
The whole leg throbbed as I hung on to the wheel. I fought to widen the
range of vision from the small hole I was boring through the mirror.

I wobbled back to check the mess. Yes, no question: Pick-up tailgates
are made for ramming. I studied the bent-up car door. I had a cheering
thought. I knew what I could do. I would go into the house and tell
Joan. I find myself cheered in unusual ways.

The affair of the Hit or Miss should have been over. I had just wrecked the side of our new station wagon, and I didn't need anything else to acknowledge that the Cosmos had punished me for my Hit or Miss lust in my heart—and mind.

But Baron, the neighbor's dog, did not agree with my philosophical surrender. The German Shepherd who spent his life on the end of a chain, tethered to his dog house, had chosen to break loose.

As I dejectedly hobbled towards the house, Baron, no doubt mentally humming "Born Free," threw his big paws against my back.

I stabbed the crutches down to catch my balance. One tip found the only fissure in the driveway surface and wedged in tightly. I yanked to pull loose, to find my balance, but Baron sent me reeling. I heard the wooden crutch snap and then my big toe, left unprotected through the open cast, went *Crack.*

I crawled towards the house, up the steps and then fell through the door. "Joan!" I cried out as I lay across the threshold. "I wrecked the car! I broke my crutch! I broke my toe."

And then I called for help. Baron who had disappeared, re-appeared on my back. I pulled the door shut against my body as he rushed the door. Baron, held back by his shoulders, pushed his head through and met my snapping dog and Joan, swinging her broom. The broom pounded the big dog off my back, then out the door. Most of Joan's whacks found their mark. The few that missed Baron hit my head. Her average was still pretty good, all things considered.

When things settled down, I thought about my Karmic tie to the Hit or Miss. I had paid dearly for my obsession with the machine, but now my thinking began to change. If I had paid for her psychically, perhaps I had paid in full. Perhaps I owned her now.

With block and tackle, prybars and levers, I visited the Hit or Miss one last time. I crutched around her, pulled the junk heaped on top away, and skidded the old car parts free of her base. I eyed the rafters, then climbed up the corn crib's interior walls, carrying the block and tackle.

Would the beams hold the weight, I wondered, then realized that after she was hoisted, I'd have to drive the truck inside, under her, then work alongside to lower her down. If the roof comes down, I thought, weighing the risk, we'll be buried together.

The rafters sagged, the building groaned, the walls bowed inward (slightly—just slightly, I told myself) as I slowly raised her from the dirt. She had to weigh over a ton, I thought as I backed the pick-up inside the corn crib and beneath the hanging engine.

I lowered her down. The truck's springs did not give out; the tires did not blow.

Then I freed her of the chains.

In the subdued light filtering through the corn crib slates, I could see the Hit or Miss looking at me.

Looking at me and grinning.

Roofing With A Naked Lady

◆

The class climbed to the roof, one student at a time, cautiously and safely, as I had taught them. The group was up there now, all of them, even the kids who the day before had showed their awful fear of heights.

But why were they out of sight on the *far* side of the roof? I wondered. And why were they so quiet? There were no sounds. They were never this quiet. On a roof, in a classroom, you do not expect quiet from teenagers; it is an unnatural state of being.

Ordinarily, I was the first one on the roof, but I had broken my foot the night before and the cast slowed me down. While I struggled to get out of the truck, the kids had removed the ladder from the rack, set it in place, and were waiting to start. Fussing with my crutches and tool belt, I gave them the sign to go ahead. They were learning; the ladder looked secure and pitched at the right angle.

I fumbled around the base of the ladder, decided to leave my crutches at the bottom, then crawled up, using my good left foot on one rung, then my right knee on the next. Maybe this isn't such a good idea, I thought. The new break was throbbing. I felt a little dizzy, and the climb was taking forever.

I pulled my weight up the ladder, rung by rung, on to the roof's eave, then clawed my way up to the ridge. When I looked over the peak, some of the kids on the other side, turned towards me, put their index finger to their lips and went, "Shhhh."

This is new, I thought. The kids quieting the teacher? I skidded my butt a few feet closer to the class and the roof's edge, then looked down.

In the backyard, next door to where we were working, surrounded by a tall privacy fence, was a lady, a good-looking, mature lady, lying on her back, sunbathing in the nude.

She opened her eyes, stared up at us for a moment, then spun around and jumped to her feet. We caught one good fleeting look as she threw a postage stamp size towel across her shoulders and made for the house.

"Come on guys," I said to the group chattering now on the roof. "Let's concentrate on our work and get this job going." But somehow the roofing mood had vanished.

Just how do you roof with a naked lady on your mind?

The Broken Cadillac

---◆---

The roof of Tommie Sefalli's house was steeper and higher than most of the other roofs we had shingled. The boys were too concerned with hanging on and being careful to pay much attention to the two Dobermans patrolling the yard or to the black Cadillac parked inside the enclosure.

Tommie was my student and his mom had asked us to do their roof. I don't think the class knew that the Cadillac's windows were blown out and that Tommie's dad had been found shot to death in the trunk.

I had seen the Cadillac before, on my way to work. It had been parked at Steger Road and Old Torrence Ave. The car was one in a string of vehicles I had seen abandoned on that corner, usually with someone dead in the trunk; the suburban chop shop operation did not always go smoothly.

When we finished the roof, the kids admired their work and started down the ladder. Tommie hung back and I said to him, "Tommie, with your dogs down below, you'll have to clean up the yard after school."

He was looking down at the car. "I don't know why Mom keeps it," he said, looking up at me. "I never saw it from this angle before."

He looked back down at the car. "Give me a few minutes, Mr. Anderson," he said. "I'll be down in a few minutes."

The Electric Door

◆

"Just what are you doing?" asked my boss, the division coordinator, Jerry Lauritsen. He had lived in a farming community before he came to Bloom Trail and recognized the fence charger I was rigging to my hallway door. "Why are you electrifying the door? Is this some kind of a joke?" he asked. "You can't do this in a public school," he quickly added.

"I have had it up to here," I told him. "Every morning, kid gets here before I do…He does it *every* morning, Jerry."

"He does what?" he asked.

"He *urinates* on my door, Jerry," I said.

"What?"

"He whizzes on my door. He pisses on my door. He micturates. I just cleaned up the floor, otherwise you'd be standing in a puddle."

"I don't care what he does," said Jerry. "You can't wire up the door. Think of what you might do to his plumbing. You could wreck him for life. Would you want that responsibility?"

"I'll disconnect the wiring," I told him. "You've made your point but don't you think the kid might have gotten a charge out of it?" I asked.

Counseling Raymond

$\blacklozenge$

I checked my rear view mirrors and there was no one behind me or to my left. The road ahead was clear on that warm spring evening except for a lone figure. I caught a glimpse of him in my headlights, 150 feet ahead, but too close to the roadway.

Joan and I were returning from the movies with a load of kids. The resurfaced road felt smooth as glass. Brian McCleish and his auto shop students had just put new shocks, brakes, and tires on the car that afternoon, and the station wagon handled like a new car. I had watched two of Brian's students torque down the lug nuts. Pretty life and death stuff: the nuts and bolts we entrust to high school kids, I thought.

And there was that guy...I tuned out the conversations in the car. The young man near the road was dressed in white, and as the wheels rolled closer to him, I picked up on more detail. A white suit and ruffled shirt, ruffled and open at the collar. A bow tie hung off to one side, and there was a red flower in his suit coat lapel. His hair was blond and long, dingy and messed up. He was weaving, weaving or rocking in time.

And from the beginning, from the first moment I saw him, I knew what he was going to do.

He rocked, timing his moves, waiting for that exact moment, waiting for the car to be in the right place. And, when it was the way he had it pictured, he jumped and threw himself flat on his stomach, across our lane, in front of the wagon.

I tore at the wheel, and without locking the brakes, I put the car on its ear. The new brakes worked with the new tires and shocks, twisting and turning the car around the prone figure. We strained against our seat belts as the car shifted direction and settled down in the next lane.

"Did you hit him?" Joan asked. "How do you know you didn't hit him?" The words were reasonable and rational. The tone was not.

"I didn't hit him with the car," I said. "I definitely did not hit him."

I pulled the car over. The kids were silent.

I asked Joan to slide over and drive to a restaurant parking lot a few feet ahead. "This may take a while," I said as I got out of the car.

I walked back to where the young man now sat on the roadway. "I need to talk to you. You and I have to get out of the road. I'll take your arm and help you up, but I don't want you to pull me down or hurt me. I have my wife and children in the car." I extended my hand.

Anticipating a scuffle, I had taken off my glasses, and everything took on an out-of-focus, surreal look. A traffic light changed and the highway came alive. Fuzzy headlights sped toward us and I could hear the sounds of traffic as I pulled him from the road. He had the stale odor of booze, cigarettes and aftershave about him, and his smell mixed with the spring air and the fresh oil smell of the road.

I held his arm; wobbly and shaking we walked to the restaurant. "How many times did you try that?" I asked. I knew I was not the first.

"Three times, three times," he repeated, turning his head away. "You were the closest."

"I teach high school," I told him, searching for something common between us. "What is going so wrong your life that you felt you had to do this?" I asked as we walked together, arm in arm.

"Things just aren't going right."

"Were you at a dance?"

"Yeah," he said, pausing. "I got caught drinking in the washroom and...and I'm suspended again." We walked towards the restaurant.

"The counselor is going to call my mom and she's going to go nuts." I kept quiet, at least he was talking.

"The girl I took to the dance just told me to go to hell."

"Things could be worse," I said. I knew it was a stupid thing to say.

"I got kicked off the swim team today," he continued. "The coach wouldn't let me ride the bus home from the meet. He told me to walk home from Michigan City. Some jerk picked me up and I had to put up with his shit all the way home...Kicked off the team over a cigarette, a lousy cigarette. The coach is an asshole." He was talking now. "A real asshole," he added, a little too loud, as we passed through the restaurant door, arm in arm and past the employee standing there.

"Where is the manager's office?" I asked the man at the door. "I need to use his office."

"I'm the manager," the man said. "You can't use the office."

But he had already made the mistake of gesturing toward the back of the restaurant. "You can't go back there," he said, following us. "Hey! I'm talking to you."

"Phone the police," I called to him as I pushed open the office door.

"Don't worry, I will," he retorted, "You don't belong in there. I don't *want* you in there..."

The young man and I sat down and waited for the police. He told me his name.

He was Raymond.

I thought about Raymond throughout the weekend. I thought how lucky we all were that I was wide awake, that the road was empty, that Brian's students had fixed the car, and that Raymond had misjudged his jump by a few critical feet.

I thought about Raymond on Monday and called his high school in Indiana.

"Doesn't surprise me," Raymond's counselor said, after listening to the story. "The kid is a jerk. He's going nowhere. He's one of my real zeros."

"Will you call him in today and talk to him?" I asked.

"Listen," the counselor said, "you work with that type of kid over there at Bloom Trail. I don't even know if he's in school today. I'm swamped with things to do and need to talk to kids who matter."

I ended the call abruptly.

I called the school back and talked to the assistant principal. She had spoken with the police. "We're going to try very hard, Mr. Anderson," she said. "We all know Raymond, and there is a plan to help him. And incidentally," she added, "the plan excludes his counselor."

History, Artefacts, And the Underwear Tree

◆

I looked inside the truck's toolbox for a wrench, and there were the trophies the class had smuggled back from the field trip. Black ones, pink ones, blue and white ones…

I didn't know if I should use rubber gloves or a stick. I did know that I was going to "ream" the class out the next day. What if Joan had looked in there to find a screwdriver? How would I have explained all those women's panties?

I had spent enough time and effort the day before discussing the history of our area. "Our high school sits where the Sauter-Vincent log cabin once stood," I told the class. I drew a map on the blackboard and let the chalk wiggle from side to side. "Did you ever notice how Sauk Trail, the road that runs past Bloom Trail High School, winds and turns?" I asked them. "Sauk Trail does not go in a straight line. Instead it follows the highest part of the ground. The deer who made the trail, later the Indians, and then the pioneers, traveled along the highest pieces of ground."

"Why'd they do that?" Bill Myers asked.

"Because they didn't want to get their feet wet, dummy," Anthony Wells explained.

"Deer don't care if they get their feet wet," Bill said, slightly raising his voice.

"But the Indians did," Anthony returned.

"You're both making good points," I said. "But I'm trying to tell you that this area was once low and marshy and *everybody* wanted to stay dry. Back before the pioneers and early settlers came, this area saw a lot of Indian traffic."

"Where were they going?" Jim Flarity asked. His participation in group discussions was unusual. It seemed the group was *thinking*; we were "on a roll." "Did they obey the speed limit and stop for the traffic lights?" he continued.

"Did you guys ever see that chicken at East End Avenue who crosses Sauk Trail with the light?" Bill asked.

"I know that chicken!" cried Raymond, the new kid. "He waits for the light to turn green before he starts out, waits for it again when he turns the corner."

"Come on, guys," I pleaded, trying to get back on track.

"No, really!" Raymond insisted. "He really waits for the light to change. He actually does. Actually."

"Actually?" Anthony Wells mocked. "*Actually*? Pretty big word there, Ray."

"Hey," Raymond called, with a "watch-it" tone. "My father is Indian, and I probably have relatives who walked on Sauk Trail."

"Relatives?" Anthony asked. "Did their Pintos run out of gas?"

"I think he means ancestors, Anthony," I said, attempting to steer us back on course.

"No, I mean relatives," Raymond said. "I have Indian relatives on both sides of my family. My father…"

"We know, your father is an Indian, an Indian with a Pinto."

The field trip went well. We arrived at the forest preserve along Sauk Trail and marched into the woods, back to where I knew the first pioneer farm once stood. I had shown them what to look for: shard or flint chips from the Indians, broken ceramic pieces and pieces of rusty iron from the pioneers.

The class looked around the old foundation with enthusiasm, began to pick things up and put them in their pockets.

Students went exploring farther from the ruins. Some of the more adventurous were out of sight; I wondered if I could get them all back. Their parents had signed the standard field trip form: "I give my son or daughter <*Fill in Blank*> permission to blah-blah-blah-and-blah. I assume all responsibility, and absolve the school from blah-blah-blah-and-more-blah. Signed: Ronnie's Mom, <*Your Name Here*>."

But I didn't want to come back and make that telephone call, "Mrs. Ronnie's Mom, I left Ronnie in the woods. I called him and he wouldn't come out. We looked for him for at least four minutes before the bus had to leave."

There was a cry from the woods: "Hey, Guys! Come over here. We found something really neat; you got to come over here. Hurry up!"

The field trip was a success, I thought. We were finding stuff. *Neat* stuff. "Let's go over and see what they found," I said to the small group still hanging around me. They had first poked the old foundation ruins with sticks but were now sword fighting.

"Isn't it something," Jim Flarity announced, admiring the underwear tree. "I found it all by myself."

"You can have it," Arthur Wells told him. "It's just a bunch of girls' underwear in a tree."

"It's an artifact, Mr. Anderson," Jim protested. "Can we bring them back to the school?"

"No, Jim," I said. "It is not an artifact. Leave them alone; you don't know where they've been."

"Of course we know where they've been," said Anthony.

"They've been on girls. They are girls' underwear."

"But how did they get here?" Bill Myers asked.

"Some guy does chicks here, dummy!" Anthony said.

"Lots of chicks, sometimes more than one at a time. He gets to keep their underwear."

"Look at all the undergarments," declared Raymond, the new kid.

"Un-*der*-gar-*ments*. Pretty big word there, Ray," Anthony mocked.

"Hey!" said Raymond, "it's a perfectly good word…"

"We know, it's an Indian word. You learned it from your father."

"Your father with the Pinto!" yelled another kid.

I looked at the small bush hung with the underwear. "The field trip is over." I declared. "We have to get back. Don't forget to bring the stuff you found so we can mount it on a board."

The group staggered off through the woods, away from the underwear tree. Someone started to chant, "Un*Der*Gar*Ment*…Un*Der*Gar*Ment*…" The chanting grew louder; it gained volume as more and more voices were added. I found myself wanting to chant along.

"I forgot my lighter, I'll be right back," Anthony called, turning back toward the underwear tree base camp.

"You're not supposed to have a lighter in school," Raymond, the new kid, said.

"It's not a lighter. It's *kind* of a lighter but it's not a lighter…and we're not in school," Anthony called back. He was already gone.

We boarded the bus. "It was a great field trip, Mr. Anderson," the kid sitting next to me said. "Why couldn't we bring our sticks on the bus?"

"Oh, look!" called Bill Myers, "It's the chicken at East End Avenue. He's waiting for the light to turn."

"Stop the bus," hollered Anthony. "I *want* that chicken."

The Drive Through the School:
Education to Go

◆

The red Pinto stood in a pool of its own oil. A trail of twisted aluminum channel and broken glass littered the floor. Bent metal-framed chairs sat on its hood and surrounded its nose. The car's left fender gently touched the wall as Angelo, the custodian, reached in through the open car door and shut down the knocking engine. He stepped back and looked at the destruction, then left to call his boss. It would take more than a broom to clean up this mess.

Several hours later, I stood with a small group looking at the car resting in the hallway. The metal and the broken glass lying in the dark oil reflected the light coming from the hole in the building. I could feel the cold morning air as the school was invaded by a west wind.

"What time did you find it, Angelo?" I asked.

"About 6:30 this morning," he answered. "It was still running, you know. Chugging right along. Over-heating and knocking, but still running."

"Anybody inside?" I asked.

"Nope," he replied. "For awhile I was worried I might find the driver here, inside the building, but I think he's gone. Fred, why are you here on a Saturday morning?"

"Just lucky," I answered. "I came to drop off some lumber I'll need on Monday. I wouldn't have missed this for the world. What do you think he was trying to do?" I asked.

"Oh, he was trying to drive the car through the building; in one end, and out the other," Angelo replied. "He would have made it, hadn't been for all these chairs."

"Why are the chairs in the hall?"

"So we could scrub out the eating area. Now some of them are wedged under the car, stopped it dead, and tore out the oil pan."

A tow truck backed up to the opening in the wall. I heard the truck's door slam, then the driver appeared at the hole. He dragged a cable with him. Kicking a remaining piece of the aluminum out of his path, he stopped and looked at the car. "You'll never figure out who did this," he stated. "The car has got to be stolen. And will you look at this? It took out two sets of doors, and the windshield's not even broken."

The tow truck driver attached his hook to the car, then reeled the Pinto backwards through the hole. I looked at the destruction one more time before I left to unload my lumber.

What a stupid stunt, I thought. What a waste of an automobile.

What a fantastic piece of driving.

The Santa Claus Man

---◆---

Dorothy Clark called me on the radio from her station at the switchboard. "Fred, what's your location?"

"Go ahead, Dorothy," I returned, "I'm on the second floor."

"There's an older man at the door. He's wandering back and forth between the front entrance and the outside office windows. I talked to him through the glass but got no response. I think he's lost."

I was checking to see that the building was empty and that classroom doors were locked. I told her I'd be right down.

An old man stood outside. I watched him for a moment from my place inside the building, behind the locked glass door. He wore a pair of new tan work shoes and rocked from side to side. His green pants were held up by red suspenders. He wore no jacket over his white shirt. The hair on his head and his full beard were bushy and snow-white. His dull blue eyes looked away as I came closer.

"Can I help you?" I inquired as I opened the door. "Who do you need to see?"

There was no response. "Can I help you?" I asked again. Again, he did not speak.

I rephrased my question again, and then again. Each time there was no response from him. He gave no indication he understood anything I was saying.

Dorothy came out to help. She had shut down her switchboard and was wearing her coat. "Are you having any luck, Fred?" she asked. She could tell I wasn't.

"He looks like Santa Claus," she whispered.

Dorothy and I tried a gentle interrogation, changing the format of our questions to him each time. We felt if we could find the magic set of words, we might turn on some light in his mind that had been temporarily turned off. The method did nothing to help us unravel the mystery of what he wanted, who he was, or where he came from.

It was my first experience with what must have been Alzheimer's disease, and I believe it was Dorothy's, too. I took the Santa Claus man to the toilet where he remembered how to relieve himself. Dorothy fired up her switchboard and found a social service agency, who, after several hours, came and took him to their facility.

My experience with the Santa Claus man later helped me cope with my mother's illness and then my aunt's. Mom and Aunt Lil were brilliant women, but in their early 70s, they began to forget. Later, just like small children, they could not be safely left alone. The change in their behavior was startling.

My mother wrote a check for several thousand dollars to the paper boy.

She began to hide money in tightly rolled-up pieces of paper.

She took walks and got lost.

She took the car for a drive, ended up miles from home and was returned by considerate strangers.

She began to shoplift clothing and groceries. She forgot to pay.

She wore her undergarments on the outside of her dress; this was not yet fad or fashion.

She forgot all our names and the names of our children.

She forgot my father, who was the person who cared for her each day. "Who is that man?" she asked.

She wore her shoes on the wrong feet.

She forgot her name.

She lost her mind and she lost her way.

My sister, Cris, told me that Mom made raisin coffee for her. I told her that the lasagna coffee Mom brewed in the percolator the day before was also pretty good. The family found some humor in the nightmare.

My aunt, gracious hostess that she was, served us dog food in the dog's bowl.

She placed a paper bag on the stove and began to cook us a meal.

She sent her handyman's daughter through college.

She became prey for shady investment counselors.

She was a chain smoker, until the day she forgot to smoke.

The sweet woman, who never raised her hand to anyone in anger, began to beat her little dog. He was so very confused, until my sister, Martha, rescued him. Cris found him a home.

My wife, Joan, and my mother had been close. When Mom was dying, Joan thanked her for her love and support. I watched the two of them say goodbye in the darkened bedroom and saw the vacant expression on Mom's face change. Her eyes brightened and she smiled at Joan. I hadn't seen her smile in such a long time. She started to talk. Her words were garbled but her speech had its familiar inflection; Joan knew what Mom was saying. Some lost thing returned to Mom on her last afternoon. Something in her spirit remembered.

Consumer Education

◆

Terry Burton, a special education student, said he was going into business. He had listened carefully to his teacher. "Buy low, sell high," she had told him.

Terry rode the public bus through the southern suburbs, through the South Side of Chicago, to the North Side to a novelty shop. There he bought 20 dollars worth of giant balloons at one dollar apiece.

One the way home he studied the business lesson in his mind, "Buy low, sell high," or was it, "Buy high, sell low," or, "High low, sell buy…" It was something like that.

When he returned to school the next day, he sold the dollar balloons to his classmates for fifty cents apiece.

Sales were brisk, and business was good. "I could have sold twice as many balloons as I had," Terry told his teacher. "Thanks for getting me started in business. I'm going back for more."

The Little Bomber Boy

◆

I listened to the kids' conversations, too loud and meant for me to hear,
"He shouldn't have brought it to school."
   "He shouldn't have made it."
   "He shouldn't have brought it here."

"What's going on, guys?" I asked the group talking at their work bench. First period had just begun. The whole day was ahead of us, but something was wrong. The kids looked at me, but were silent. "Tell me what's going on," I demanded, but again the kids were quiet.

"I'm going to ask you one more time," I said to them, then added. "If there is someone here at school you care about, your girlfriend, a brother or sister, tell me what you are talking about. Right now!"

One of the kids looked me directly in the eye and said softly, "Go look in Ryan Blakley's locker."

Little Ryan Blakley? my mind questioned. The kid wasn't big enough to cause anyone trouble. But I called the office and found that Ryan's locker was just down the hall from my shop classroom.

The class was working quietly now; I left them for a moment to open Ryan's locker with my pass key. I stared at the contents inside.

Good Lord! I was over my head on this one.

Inside the locker were packages loosely wrapped in brown paper. Fuses trailed down over the top shelf. I carefully closed the locker door and called the office once again.

"I think you need to call the bomb squad," I said to our principal.

"How did you find this stuff, Anderson?" Officer Rewers asked as he carefully removed the packages. "If this is what we think it is, there is enough plastics here to blow off one end of the building."

"Just lucky," I told him. "What do you suppose the kid was going to do?" I asked.

"We have him in custody now," he said, "and he says he was going to do the urinals in the washrooms. This stuff would have taken out more than the johns. Good work, Anderson."

I watched the men as they carried the basket down the hall toward the truck parked in front, and then returned to my classroom to relieve the substitute teacher the front office had sent.

"What's going on?" one of the kids quietly asked.

"The stuff is gone," I told him softly. "We don't have to worry about it anymore."

"What stuff?" he asked.

"We don't want anyone to know we knew anything," the other added.

"Don't worry," I told them. "Nobody asked, and I don't plan to tell. But you did the right thing. Sometimes you have to speak up. Let's see if we can get back to business and get the shop cleaned up."

Later that day, God knows why, Ryan was released in the custody of his parents. He then went home, fired up his home lab, and blew the fingers off both of his hands.

I saw him when he returned to school after a two week suspension. Black thread sutured up the stubs of his fingers.

I saw him again, two years later as he roared into a gas station on a big '74 Harley chopper. His 100 pound frame straddled the bike; his feet hardly touched the ground and it looked as if he hadn't grown at all since his sophomore year in high school.

"Ryan, how ya doin'?" I called to him. "That big bike giving you any trouble?"

"Nah, I miss a shift now and then," he answered, holding up his hands, showing me his stubby half-fingers.

"Looks like they healed up pretty well," I said, walking closer to Ryan and his machine.

"Yeah," he said, "I have a hard time grabbin' the throttle. And the front brake? Forget it!"

"You still doin' chemistry?" I asked.

"No more chemistry," he replied, shoving the gas nozzle into the tank and somehow pulling the trigger. "Good seein' you, Mr. Anderson."

"Good seeing you. Ryan," I told him returning to my own gas tank needs.

The Kid Who Knew it All

◆

"Let's go into Mr. Hein's Body Shop," I told Freddie Tinker. "He's eating lunch this period and won't mind if we use his paint shaking machine."

"Okay," Freddie answered enthusiastically, "I didn't want to mix'er up by hand." He had finished building his saw horse, insisted on a special paint color, and as he told me, it was time to "paint'er up."

"And whatever you do, don't touch the car Mr. Hein's class just finished," I emphasized as we walked through my office passage to the body shop. "Isn't the finish on that car beautiful!" I exclaimed when we got to the spray booth next to the paint shaker. The car glistened through the open door, and I could see there was a lot of Tom Hein in this job. His students had started the body work but Tom had brought it to a point that only a trained professional could. He had applied the paint just wet enough to create that high gloss look, and there were no sags or runs.

"I know how to paint cars," Freddie said. "I know all 'bout that stuff."

"Shake the paint five or six minutes," I told Freddie. "It's been sitting around for awhile, and the pigment has settled to the bottom."

"I know," he told me.

"And whatever you do, do not touch the car," I repeated.

"I know," Freddie continued. "I'll be careful. I'll mix'er-up, then paint'er-up. I'll be careful." I started to show Freddie the timer switch and how to clamp the paint in the machine but he told me, "I know how to do it. You don't have to show me. I know how. I know all about…"

I left him alone with his paint and returned to my shop.

"Mr Anderson!" Freddie shouted from my office door, "There's been a horrible accident."

I turned to look at the kid. His clothes were covered with paint and his safety glasses streaked. He was a different color.

"What the he…What happened? Are you okay?"

"I put the paint on the machine," he cried, "clamped'er down, turned 'er on, and the cover came off. There's paint all over! It's all over everything!"

"How about the car?" I asked. I think I knew the answer.

"It got'er too," he moaned. "It's all over ever'-thing!"

I left Freddie in my shop, dripping by the sink, walked around his footprints on my office rug and went to visit the mess. The paint can was empty. It was clamped in the machine, but sideways with the clamps, designed to hold the top lid and bottom of the can, pressing on the round curved sides. The lid lay on the floor under a large pool of paint. The rest of the paint had been launched through the open spray booth door onto Mr. Hein's newly painted car.

As I helped Freddie scrub most of the blue paint out of his blond hair, I asked, "Do you know what you did wrong?"

"The paint can got in there crooked," he answered, "but something always goes wrong. My dad calls me a knucklehead."

"Well, sometimes you need to slow down and listen to instructions," I continued. "Sometimes it pays to…"

"I know, I know," he interjected.

"Let me help you wash the paint off your sleeve," I said, reaching for his shirt soaking in the sink.

"I can do it," he said. "I know how to do-er. I know how."

I left Freddie scrubbing away to return to Tom's shop and the mess on the floor. I didn't know where to start or if I should even touch the multi-colored car in the spray booth. Freddie would have known. He would have known how to "do-er."

He knew about everything.

He knew it all.

Art's Kennels

———————————— ◆ ————————————

"Your house is sitting on historic ground!" I told Chuck Savino. "No wonder your fence posts didn't rot. They are planted in special soil. Your house is built on the old location of Art's Kennels."

Chuck had called to ask if my Construction Trades Class could rebuild just the top part of his fence. From the address he gave me I knew where he lived.

"What is so special about a dog kennel?" he asked.

The "specialty" was that Art's Kennels did not raise dogs. Nor breed dogs nor train dogs or sell dogs as their sign proudly proclaimed.

Art's Kennels was a house of prostitution, or, as some might call it, a "home of commercial affection."

The whorehouse lay on the south side of Steger Road in Will County. Although Art's Kennels was close geographically to Bloom Trail High School, it remained independent of us and did not offer extracurricular programs. None of our boys was caught visiting the place, nor were job applications for the girls filed with our vocational counselor.

The proprietor of Art's must have run into difficulties with the local political-gangster/gangster-political machine, because one day, the police shut the place down. A cop later told me they'd been hiding out of sight behind the place, and had seen an old man drive up the one-lane road to the house anticipating his hour of amour.

Then he saw the squad cars. He apparently realized he could not turn his car around, so he drove into the midst of the squad cars. He got out of his car, pointed to a skinny horse in the farm field and announced in a firm voice, "I've come to buy that horse over there."

The police said they let him go out of a sense of fair play.

Don't Cut Off Your Fingers
And Other Practical Rules

◆

"Rules! Rules! Rules!" Justin Brighton exclaimed. "Everywhere you go there are more rules."

"Calm down, Justin," I told him. "Rules help us work safely in the shop."

"Why are there always ten of them?" he asked. "Why aren't there four or maybe 14? Why don't you give us some rules about stuff that happened in here?"

Okay, Justin, *these* rules are based on my experiences as a teacher.

These are simple and practical rules.

And Justin, these rules are for you.

Don't throw large chunks of metal from the balcony and break the sink.

Do not carry your gun while in class.

Don't go in the toilet with another boy and lock the door.

Don't bend a framing square into a pretzel shape.

Don't whack at a locker with a roofing hatchet.

Don't beat the walls with a hammer.

Don't pass drugs while in class.

Don't smoke between the van and the building, toilet, and blow smoke through the vent while standing on the seat into the body shop.

Don't urinate on the hallway floor.

Don't defecate along the locker room wall.

Don't hire someone to beat someone up, knock out his teeth, break his jaw and nose.

Don't steal stuff.

Don't expose yourself.

Don't run down the hall with baseball bats, braining other students, knocking them out.

Don't cut off your finger.

Don't come to class late or not at all.

Don't leave early or sleep in class and sleep through the last activity bus going home.

Don't get yourself locked in a storeroom overnight with another boy and a girl.

Don't drink wine and get sick on yourself and fall down.

Don't fight on the bus, smoke, stand up, spit, throw paper, rocks, knives or other students, break and smash out the windows, use profanity or beat up the bus driver.

Don't threaten to hijack the bus.

Don't hijack the bus, light the seats on fire, cut the seats or pull stuffing out of the seats.

Don't rub girls the wrong way without their permission.

Don't masturbate in class.

Don't eat in class and push your sandwich into someone's face.

When out of school, conduct yourself properly.

Don't throw boulders off the overpass killing drivers of automobiles.

Don't try to cut off someone's nose with a knife from your boot.

Don't rape and kill other students.

Don't set the school or your house on fire.

Don't drive your car on the school lawn or through the hallway.

Don't steal the school's American flag.

Don't shoot out the school's windows with BB guns, pistols, semiautomatic or fully automatic weapons.

Don't do drugs or party till you puke.

Don't have babies out of wedlock.

Don't kill your brothers, sisters, or parents.

Don't steal and sell your father's $100,000 coin collection for coke money.

Don't set yourself on fire or burn your arm with cigarettes.

Don't spell words wrong or use backwards S's or B's etc., when doing homemade tattoos.

Don't share dope or tattoo needles without sterilization.

Don't forget safe sex.

Don't pose for nude photos for your foster parents or parents.

Don't drink and drive.

Dog Stories

◆

I am sure most teachers bring personal stories and experiences into the classroom. I remember when I was a student in high school, if I could get this old guy talking throughout the class period, and get him to forget the clock, the test or written work would be put off until another time. He told wonderful stories and only taught from the syllabus towards the end of the semester, or when his supervisor came to visit.

I try to stay on target as I teach, but bring my stories into the classroom when I feel they fit with the curriculum. Some of them are even true. Several, in fact.

I teach the students in my woodshop how to build a small plant stand. They learn how to measure, cut and fit a half lap joint. One of the joints is cut from the top on one leg, and fits into the joint cut from the bottom of the other. Invariably, someone cuts both joints from the same side and one leg fits upside down. The student usually brings me the mistake and is all upset. I then feel it only fitting to share this classic American folk tale: "The Best Hunting Dog."

When I was a young man in…Maine, I had a hunting dog. He was the best hunting dog in the county, and people came to our small farm to watch me work my dog in the field.

One day the dog and I were hunting. He ran out of sight to retrieve a bird I'd shot, and I heard him squeal and cry out in pain. I ran over to where he lay. He had run onto a farmer's scythe left in the field, and he now lay on *both* sides of the blade, split right down the middle. I tore off my jacket, slapped the dog together and wrapped him up tightly. I carried him home and placed him next to the wood stove where he could keep warm. I poured a healing liniment on the jacket and let it soak through to heal his terrible wounds.

After a week, he tried to wag his tail that was sticking out of the jacket. He moved his mouth and whimpered, and I gave him sips of water and small pieces of food. After several weeks he was barking and trying to shed the jacket, and so I unwrapped him.

Would you believe I had put the dog together wrong way, too, just like your plant stand, Charlie. He had two legs sticking up and two legs pointing down. He was still the best hunting dog in the county. He'd run on two legs until he got tired, then flip over on the other two, barking and wagging his tail at both ends.

One kid in the class always calls out, "You made that up!"

   *   *   *

When I talk to my class about bracing, I tell them about the buildings I dismantled for materials to build my own barn. I get nostalgic when I tell this story. A kid who recognizes that faraway glassy look in my eye can be clever enough to ask the key questions. He can milk this story along and into the time set aside for the written exercise. This is the story of "Buck and the Barn":

The forest preserve condemned a group of farms and homes to expand their property The buildings were to be auctioned off for sale, but before the bidding process could begin, the bulldozers started tearing down all the good stuff. The forest preserve officers arrested anyone they caught taking materials, but still the crews were wrecking things left and right.

Every afternoon after teaching school, I would go get my big yellow Labrador Retriever, Buck. We would drive to my job site, down the long driveway to the building I was dismantling. Buck watched over me as worked. When the forest preserve officers drove back to where I was working, Buck would sound the alarm. I would retreat out of sight, Buck would bark and growl at the occupants of the car, keeping them from exiting the vehicle as I hid and waited. The police would eventually drive away and I would return to work. We made a good team, Buck and I.

The kids that lived nearby began torching old buildings on adjoining farms. As long as they could hear me working with crowbars and wrecking tools, they left that property alone and burned around me. I would work until dark, turn off the truck lights and ease down the quarter mile long driveway.

I worked for weeks, one step ahead of the bulldozers, one step ahead of the forest preserve officials and one step ahead of the kids. One night, after I went home, they burned the farmhouse down. The next day, I was fascinated to see what remained inside: a log cabin built of big hewn logs, at one time native to our area. Someone had built the newer house around the log cabin. It was charred but still intact.

I stood and watched it smoldering away that evening in the twilight. It sat next to a farm pound where a child had drowned ten years before. I thought about the number of families and lives the beautiful piece of property had touched before the forest preserve took it over for a suburban picnic grove.

The bulldozers and fire setters were closing in now. A number of people without big dogs to protect them were arrested for taking building materials. I knew I would have to finish and collect the rest of my barn. I now had the timbers and the siding, the stall partitions, gates, doors and loft planking, but I was missing the rafters and roof boards. They could be found in one old 60 feet long structure.

I tried for days to get the building to drop to the ground so I could safely work on it. All the bracing was removed and still it was standing as a skeleton. It refused to go down.

Inside the structure was one last piece of plywood nailed to the old stall planks. I knew that piece of plywood was the key to the puzzle and I tiptoed inside the shaky structure with a chain and hook. It was a calculated risk, I thought, as a light breeze stirred the building and moved the roof now over my head. If it went down now, no one would ever find me.

I attached the hook to the plywood, slipped out with the other end of the chain, secured it to the truck's bumper and with the truck gave it a mighty tug. The barn settled halfway down to the ground.

It was stuck, halfway up and halfway down. The building was under stress and the roof planking was bent and bowed. I got up on top of the roof and started to pull the planks, one by one, from the rafters. When I removed the nails, each plank snapped out of place. I was careful not to get hit in the face as I worked, or the crotch, an equally important area, but was unprepared for what was to happen.

One last board held everything together and when I pulled it loose, the building started down. I stood on the crest of a giant wooden wave and then in the valley. Up and down the building snaked, as I stood with my knees bent to absorb the shock, my arms to my sides for balance.

Buck watched from a safe distance, and when the building was finally down, he leaped up on the roof that had settled in the dust. His tail was wagging.

And that is the story of how the barn came down and how a 4x8 piece of plywood braced the whole structure.

"Remember," I tell the class, "buildings are built with triangular bracing for strength."

"I'm sorry guys. I took up so much time with the story, the period is almost over. There won't be time for the written assignment."

Cooking With Joan And Nan

◆

When Nan Conners was not teaching sewing skills, fabricating aprons and Cinderella dresses, she was teaching cooking and showing some pretty inept kids the secrets of her kitchen. Nan never wanted this story told and my wife, Joan, never wanted the story told…

Now it can be told.

Not once upon a time, but one school day, Joan substituted for Nan. The first part of the day went pretty well. Nan's lesson plans were clear and well organized, and the work kept the classes busy most of the period. But then came Nan's "less than best" class. Joan found it a major classroom control trick just keeping everyone in their seats. One student stood out as the kid she would really have to keep her eye on. Nan had left a seating chart and Joan quickly learned his name.

Ryan Johnson was not only difficult for a teacher to get along with but he was also unloved by the rest of the class. Near the period's end, Ryan cried out, "Someone took my gym shoes. I can't leave without my gym shoes!"

"Let's all help Ryan look for his shoes," Joan directed the class. "Everyone start looking. Are you sure you brought them to class?" she asked, looking at the clock.

"He forgets his stuff all the time," someone said.

"He loses things. He probably didn't bring his shoes to class," said another student. "He's absent minded, Mrs. Anderson," the first student said.

"I want my shoes. I'll fail gym if I don't dress today!" Ryan cried in desperation as the bell sounded for the period's end. "Don't let the class go," he whined, making one last attempt to get his shoes. But Joan let the class loose to get to their next period and left Nan a class report about the shoe problem.

The next day when Nan returned and fired up the ovens—the rest is gourmet *shoe*ffle history. The smell of burned rubber wafted throughout all the halls.

Cooking With Fred

◆

I lit myself on fire one day in the food lab. I'd been asked to disconnect the older model gas stoves and hook up the new ones donated to the program by Commonwealth Edison. I went to the home economics room with my tools and a student helper accompanied me. We disconnected the old units and pushed them out of the way, slipped the new stoves into place, and connected them to the gas source. I used my little bottle of soap suds and a brush to check for gas leaks, plugged the stoves into the outlets, and set the clocks.

I turned on a burner and lowered my ear to listen for escaping gas. "What is that 'click, click' sound?" I asked Nan, who'd been watching my progress.

"Watch yourself, Fred!" she said. "You're too close! It has an electronic ignition."

But before I could respond to her warning, the stove ignited with a "Whoooof!" I felt heat on my cheek and heard my hair crackling. My eyelashes, beard, mustache and the hair on my head were ablaze.

My student helper and Nan beat the fire out of me with rolled up newspapers. "The fire is out! It's out!" I shouted, as the student and Nan alternately smacked away on my burned head.

Been There, Done That

———————◆———————

I hate to go back and retrieve something I forgot. I cringe at the thought of retracing my steps, covering the same territory I covered before. Although I work with check lists, there have been times that a student or I have forgotten some tool or material back at the high school as we left for the job site. I have had to hastily return to the shop and retrieve the item before the school bus left with my student crew.

My own children are responsible and keep track of their belongings but we all forget things once in awhile. I hate to hear the words, "I forgot my glasses at Aunt Lil's, Dad. Can we please go back?" I cringe at the thought of turning the car around, following the same road backwards to where we came from. But we have gone back to pick up watches, purses, baby dolls and jackets.

I hate to discover I forgot to buy a gallon of milk at the grocery store. I cringe at the thought of returning to the store, to the milk aisle and back to the long "ten item or less" check-out counter. But I have gone back, stood in line counting all the items in the basket in front of me, estimating how long it will take to get back up there and finally out the door again. I'll stand on one foot then another, shifting my weight, seething about the time I have lost. But I have learned to breathe slowly and deeply to calm down, and I find I can put things into perspective by remembering Grandma Fries.

When Joan's grandmother, Caroline Fries, approached the end of her 99th year, she asked that the formality of using the name "Grandmother" be abandoned. She said she longed to hear her first name. She loved the sound of it and now that all her friends and older relatives were gone she never heard the music of her name, Caroline, anymore.

Caroline told us she never felt any older than 16 in her mind and in her heart. She felt she was still the young girl who tried and tried to come to America. Caroline had a brief encounter with the Gypsies in Europe and with some help from them hid on a boat sailing to America. She was discovered as a stowaway minutes before it sailed. The authorities returned her to the relatives who continued to work her long hours, night and day, at their tavern-restaurant in Austria.

When Caroline later came to America, she was sponsored by an aging aunt in Milwaukee. She told us of the rough crossing, terrible storms, sea sickness, poor rations and crowded conditions on the boat. She described her joy at first seeing the Statue of Liberty and the long wait at Ellis Island. But she was with her younger brother, her one close family member, and the fact that they were together softened the hardship of the trip.

But it's this story of Caroline's that helps me feel better if I am inconvenienced by some small extra trip I might have to make:

*   *   *

Caroline arrived at her aunt's home in Milwaukee after that long trip with her brother. The aunt told her that she did not want the younger boy, she had not bargained for him, he was not a part of the contract, and so, Caroline would take him back to Europe.

Caroline took him home. She reversed the long trip by wagon and train and boat, to Europe and to Austria where she said goodbye to her brother forever and returned across the sea, to the Statue of Liberty, to Ellis Island and to Milwaukee where she worked for years to pay back her aunt for the multiple passages to and from and to America.

Caroline held on to her sharp mind for all of her 99 years. She told us wonderful stories. I like the "Coming to America" story best and I wished I had known it when I was sixteen. I could have told it to my father who left the family dog, Barney, tied to a tree at a rest stop, 75 miles back from where we had driven. Barney was still there waiting and wagging his tail but my father was not in his best mood. If he had known Caroline's story—she was still "Grandma" at the time—the trip back and forth might have been more mellow. After all, 75 miles in a car is not very far.

Clock

◆

I found the clock during a gentle morning rain. It was slightly damp, resting on top of some rubbish. I glanced around to see if the neighbors were watching, then reached in their garbage can.

I held it in my hand. The cord was intact, and the plug looked safe. I took it to my shop at school were I popped the works from its case, set the innards aside to dry, then wiped the condensation from inside its dial.

When it had dried, I reassembled it and plugged it into the wall outlet in my office. It ran quietly, then sounded its raspy voice every two minutes. When I was satisfied that it worked well, I put it away in my desk drawer where I forgot it for a while.

Later that week, I had a talk with Tim Boyd, a favorite student of mine. I knew that Tim wanted to be a carpenter like his dad. His written and practical work in class was wonderful—but his attendance was terrible. Unless things changed drastically, graduation was not in his future.

"Tim, why is your attendance so bad?" I asked. "You seem to have trouble getting to school. What is the problem?"

"I have no way to wake up." he replied. "My dad goes to work before I am supposed to get up, and my mom sleeps late. I just can't seem to get up on my own. I know I miss too much school."

"I've got just the thing for you," I said, as I reached in the desk drawer and handed him the clock. "Thanks! Mr. Anderson," he exclaimed. "I'll put it right next to my bed. I'll start using it tomorrow." He wound up the cord and took it away.

For weeks he came to school everyday. And almost everyday he thanked me for the thing, until one day he just stopped coming. He showed up after a long absence. He had missed too much school now: he would not graduate.

"What happened?" I asked. "I haven't seen you for a while. Did the clock stop working?"

"No, it still works," he answered. "It woke me up every morning, but then I discovered the snooze alarm feature. The thing keeps buzzing and buzzing, waking and waking me. I keep falling asleep, until it's too late for me to get to school."

"Maybe you should throw it in the garbage can," I told him, then realized, that was probably why the thing was in the garbage can to begin with.

Justice

◆

I looked at the faculty bulletin:

There would be cheerleader practice today.

Chess Club was meeting after school.

Tom Jackson was dead.

He had passed away in his sleep the day before.

It had been only last year that I saw Tom at the district teachers' meeting. He had looked around to see if we were alone. "Fred," he said softly, "I wanted to talk to you before we went into the faculty meeting. Do you remember the time Sonny Allen hurt me?"

Tom would be retiring in a month. I hadn't seen him since he'd been reassigned to our sister campus.

"I remember, Tom," I said. "The kid broke your glasses and bloodied your nose. That was quite a day..."

Tom knew I'd remember. Tom Jackson taught in the Opportunity Adjustment Program. The school removed kids with behavioral problems like Sonny from the rest of the school to two portable trailers in the parking lot. That proved to be still too close to the school.

"That was the day four of our kids got in the main building, ran through the halls with clubs and brained anyone in their path," Tom stated.

I nodded. When the passing bell rang, there were kids lying all along the shop hallway, the hallway past the business rooms and along the hall of the science wing...

"How many kids did they hurt?" Tom asked.

I was never sure, but we found kids on their knees holding their heads, kids lying on their stomachs, kids on their backs, kids leaning against lockers, trying to steady themselves. We walked and wheeled a bunch of them to the nurse's office...We had kids lying down any place there was room. I know the ambulances made multiple runs to the hospital.

"You know," Tom said, "Sonny did more than bloody my nose. He broke it and chipped two of my teeth. I thought I knew the kid well enough to stop him, but he sucker punched me. It took a long time to get over that one."

Tom's voice trailed off, and then he quietly said, "I got him, Fred. The court never did enough, but I got the son of a bitch. It cost me 50 dollars, and it was worth every penny."

Tom looked around again to assure himself our conversation remained private. "I sat in a car across the street and after the guy I hired knocked out all of Sonny's front teeth and broke his nose, the guy walked over to my car and asked, 'Is that enough?' I said it was. I paid him and then I went home. Sonny...The kid's in jail now for murder. Did you know that?"

"Yeah, Tom," I said. "I bet every time he runs his tongue along the space where his teeth used to be, he'll remember the one last lesson you taught him."

"He doesn't know it was me," declared Tom. "Do you think I'm nuts? I've kept this quiet all these years, but I'm retiring soon and I just wanted someone to know. I wanted someone to know I didn't take it lying down."

Now, a day in school, I held the announcements of cheerleader practice and Chess Club and Tom Jackson's death. I read over the funeral arrangements and a brief account of Tom's service to the district.

I wondered if anyone else knew his secret, knew he had paid Sonny back.

"Is that enough?" Tom's hired hitman had asked.

It was.

It was justice.

The Bird Trap

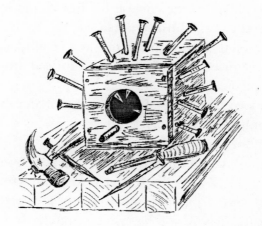

Shawn Travis kept to himself, quietly doing his paperwork. A black zippered notebook lay open on his work bench. Pens, pencils, and a ruler were arranged and attached on the inside cover like carefully cared for instruments.

Although he turned in his written work, often adorned across the top and side margins with sketches of stick figures, nonsensical symbols, and other strange marks, he neglected to work on assigned woodworking projects. He dressed always in dark trousers and a black tee shirt; I thought he might be too particular about his clothes. I had talked to him about wearing a work apron and getting down to business with the rest of the class, but each time I'd have this conversation with him, he would bend down to wipe the shop dust from his black dress shoes and avoid my eyes.

I was encouraged, one afternoon, to see Shawn working on a project of his own; perhaps I could work out a passing grade for him after all.

Shawn was building a six inch hollow cube from scraps of plywood he found in the shop. He drilled a one-inch diameter hole in one side and then drove nails he had sharpened on the grinder, through the sides, angling them toward the center.

When I asked him what the box was for, he told me, looking at me for the first time, that it was a bird trap. He said the bird would get inside, get frightened, then thrash around inside and get impaled on the sharpened spikes. He showed me a feature I had missed: holes drilled along the bottom of the box for blood drainage.

I talked to Shawn's counselor, Del Mach, about Shawn's interest in the bird trap. He pulled Shawn's file, dropped it on his desk, then studied the information for a moment.

"Fred," he said, "I could suggest that we find an interest for the kid, to give him some direction, perhaps part-time employment. But the file says he already has a job. He works for a mortician after school, embalming bodies. I think you have to be content to provide him with additional vocational training."

"Okay," I agreed, "but does he have a work permit?"

"The question is, Fred," Del countered, "does Shawn Travis have a trapping permit?"

Meet the Family

◆

I could feel the turmoil as I approached the pay phone in the front foyer. The girls were yelling at each other, oblivious that anyone was around or that they were yelling near the office.

"Fuck you, you mother fuckin' bitch!" Yolanda Brown screamed. "Fuck you and your whole mother fuckin' family! You ain't touchin' *nothin'* of mine. You keep your little whore hands to yourself. Understand, bitch?"

"I ain't takin' no more of your shit!" Diane Moore screamed back. "You're why I got suspended. I called home, and when my mother and older brother get here, your ass is dead and so is the dean's. And don't you talk about my family. My family is going to see me through this bullshit. You hear, bitch?"

Jim Jankus, Diane's dean, was in the office. I could see him through the glass and I wanted to warn him that Diane Moore's mother and brother were on the way. I started for the office door just as Diane's family entered the building from the street.

"He's inside the office," Diane shouted.

"Jim," I called, moving toward him, "there's someone…"

Diane's family burst through the office door. "What is this bullshit?" Diane's mother screamed. She swept her hand across the counter top, clearing the sign-in clip boards to the floor. A second pass launched the office rhododendron into the air. The pot hit the floor and the plant rolled on the rug, stripped of its dirt.

I turned away from Jim and faced the noise. He had moved behind the counter into the small hallway leading to the principal's office. Diane's brother jumped over the mess and rushed along the counter toward me and the opening.

This guy is not going to stop, I thought. I could see his fist cocked back, then his knuckles flying toward my face. I twisted my head to the side and the blow grazed my cheek. The man was using my body as a ladder now, climbing over me to get through the narrow opening and to Jim.

I turned to see that he was driving Jim backwards into the wall.

I'm not going to let him get away with this, I thought as I charged and hit his back with my chest. If I could get a "full Nelson" on him, turn on the pressure to force his head down to shut off his windpipe, I could say good night to the son of a bitch.

I pushed my hands through the tangle of the two men's arms and worked my fingers up the back of his neck. But I could not push my fingers past the restriction to get a good purchase on his head.

Entangled, the three of us rolled backwards and hit the wall. I felt a stab of pain shoot through my shoulder and heard the drywall crack. We lunged forward into the first wall. Jim is going to feel this one, I thought. I heard him groan in agreement as we made impact.

We careened back and forth off those hallway walls, breaking and cracking as we went, until we slid into a heap on the floor.

Diane's mother was screaming at me, "My baby, my baby! You're hurting my baby. Let him go, let him go!"

Her shoes danced around my head as we writhed on the floor. No doubt it was the instinctive protective dance of motherly love. She was trying to get into position for a good kick.

Then I thought, *Maybe she has a gun in her purse.* I knew what a gun sounded like when it went off close by and I dreaded the feeling as I anticipated that sound.

A second pair of shoes appeared by my face on the floor. Someone was controlling Diane's mother and moving her out of the way. I heard a woman identify herself as a police officer and place Diane's mother under arrest.

I fought to hold on, struggling for a better hold and then felt cold steel banging on my wrist. "You've got the wrong hand!" I shouted. "If you're going to cuff someone, get the right guy!"

The handcuff hit me again, then again. "That's the wrong wrist!" I hollered. This was definitely not television police work; the perp was not being restrained. The good guy was being—annoyed.

"I got him now," the policewoman said. "I've got one wrist, let him go…"

"I can't let him go," I gasped. "He'll take another crack at Jim and beat me with the loose handcuff!"

We remained like that, tangled up on the floor, exhausted and unwilling to release our holds on one another. I heard police sirens in the background and Jim's muffled voice from under the guy's chest. Jim was trying to say something. "Hold on Jim," I called, "we're almost out of here."

I hung on with my fingertips, slipping, then regaining control for what seemed an eternity. Finally I felt my arms pulled through the tangle. I was free. I slid over to the side and watched Diane's brother pulled off Jim. He kicked at the police and flailed his arms. The loose handcuff clobbered the wall. I was right, I thought, he could have nailed me with the cuff.

The police flipped him over and one policeman ground his knee into the man's back. *Click, click, click,* went the handcuffs, it was a done deal, yet the man continued to fight. *Click, click,* the sound repeated as the cuffs found their mark on his wrist and ankle bones.

"They're too tight!" Diane's brother screamed. "You've got to loosen them."

"If you weren't such an asshole," the policeman said, "they could have *stayed* loose. Now you can wear them this way."

I tried to stand but my eyes couldn't hold the room together and my legs started to buckle. I put my back against the wall, slid down again on the floor, and attempted to focus on Jim, sitting against the opposite wall. My heart was pounding and I could hardly make him out.

"How you doin' over there?" I asked, carefully pronouncing my words.

"I'll be okay," he said. "I'm just shaken up. Thanks, Fred…Are you all right?"

"Yeah, I'll be okay if I can catch my breath," I said, trying to believe my words; I was not feeling well at all.

"Do you know him?" he asked. "I don't even know what that was about…"

"That was Diane Moore's brother," I answered. "Her mom was here too, and I think we just met her family." I was starting to come around. I felt good enough to say it. "Jim, it's great when the whole family takes an interest in a kid's education. We just met the Moore family and we had a family conference."

Don't Touch Me With That Thing

◆

"Fred Anderson?" the man asked as I entered the office. He had been talking to Lynn Manning, our assistant principal.

"Yes," I replied. He extended his arm. He was holding an envelope.

"What is that?" I asked.

"It's a subpoena," the man answered.

"No way!" I exclaimed, vaulting over the counter into the inner office. "I don't *want* a subpoena. I didn't do anything."

"I have to hand it to you," he said, "and you have to accept it."

"I don't know what it's for," I replied, "and I don't want it."

"We're going to give you and Jim Jankus a day off," Lynn Manning said, "so you can go to court. You remember the attack that occurred several months ago in the office."

Yes, I did remember. I had reason to.

"The State of Illinois passed a law, Fred, making it a felony to hit teachers or school officials while they are at their job. Congratulations! The State feels that you were the first teacher assaulted after the law was put in place."

"Would that guy be better off if he hit before the law was passed?" I asked, looking at the envelope.

"This man is in trouble," she replied. "He's looking at some serious jail time. The Assistant State's Attorney met with me and stressed the importance of this case," she continued. "I know you and Jim will cooperate."

"Sure I'll cooperate," I said to her. My shoulder still hurt from hitting the wall.

I wanted to again meet the guy who had done this to me.

Court would be a good place.

Questions And Answers

◆

The lawyer fumbled through his briefcase, attending to some last minute detail. Crumpled pieces of paper spilled onto the table. The man straightened his notes and attempted to organize his work.

Diane's brother and his family sat in the front row. They were looking around the courtroom, and I wondered if any of them recognized Jim and me as key players in this drama. The group had dressed as if they were in church, but their lawyer looked as if he had slept in his car—or under it. The man looked worn and wrinkled.

"The aisle-way," he began, "the aisle leading back to the office, the inner office, is very narrow, is that correct?"

"No," I answered.

"By saying 'No,' you are telling us it is narrow," he stated.

"No, I am telling you it is wide."

"The aisle-way has only enough room, just enough room, for one person to pass at a time, is that correct?" he asked.

"No," I answered again.

"In saying 'No,' are you saying there is only room for one person to pass?" His voice rose slightly.

"There is room for three people to pass. The aisle is seven feet wide," I said.

The man paused, then continued, "When you were struck," he paused again, "you were not hurt. Is that correct?"

"No, I was hurt," I told him.

"But not hurt enough to receive medical attention, is that correct?" he quickly added.

"I received medical attention and I continue to receive medical attention."

"How would you describe your injuries?"

"Your client broke the wall in three places with my body!" I described.

There were no further questions.

I found some relief from the pain in my shoulder after that day in court. I found further comfort in the news from the police. There would be no opportunity for Diane's brother to meet with Jim or me during the next five to seven years, unless I perhaps made vacation plans to visit him in the State Penitentiary.

The Time Traveler

◆

Greg Zipprich is a time traveler.

I sat straight up in bed the other night with the revelation.

Greg Zipprich was my friend and fellow teacher—and...

He is a time traveler! Now everything made sense. I understood why Greg builds large electronic machines. He designs them in the drafting room, solders the wires in the physics lab, and machines metal parts in the metal shop. He installs his devices in beautifully crafted walnut and mahogany cases he builds in my woodshop.

Rows of flashing lights, connected to switches and dimmers, are driven by magic circuitry. Greg claims his machines are designed to show the workings of a transistor to his physics classes or to illustrate the different frequencies of the sound spectrum by separating them into various colors.

Right.

Oh, I had wondered what he really did with his machines, but now I know: he messes with time. Greg seems to have time or finds time or makes time in his busy day to construct his pieces of wizardry. He messes with time, all right.

Greg has a diabetic condition that he keeps under control with regular testing, insulin, and diet. Earlier this year, he went to see his brother in Southern Illinois. When he never arrived and was long overdue, the police were asked to look for him along the interstate. They found his car abandoned, but in good condition, midway between his home and the home of his brother. An extensive search revealed Greg in a farmer's barn some distance from his car, commiserating with some sheep.

He was, according to the police, "disoriented." The police had nothing to say about the sheeps' mental condition or how they felt about commiserating by Greg.

Greg maintains that an insulin imbalance was responsible for his lapse of memory and for his inability to account for his trip away from the car. *I* suggest at this point that Greg stopped his car to rest, fired up his flashing light machine, the one he was bringing to his brother for show and tell, experienced time travel, and ended up in the barn. Something mystical happened to him that day. He returned from his experience even a more intriguing person than he was before.

Recently I saw him hovering in a chair mounted on a platform, levitating a few inches above the floor. He was slipping and sliding between two hallway walls. A group of fascinated physics students watched and waited their turn for a ride.

Greg said it was a hover craft.

He said it was plugged into the wall.

Just like he said the trip to the barn was from an insulin imbalance.

Last week I found the makings of a new time machine in the dumpster. It started out as a discarded broken exercise bike but when I gave it to Greg he added parts. He welded a bracket to the frame and fit a car generator to the wheel through a series of jack shafts and pulleys. He added some lights (submitted for your consideration: again, the lights!) and a car radio tuned to an "oldies station" (no clue there!).

When I sat on the bike to give it a try, Greg said, "Don't pedal too fast, Fred. I still have a few bugs to work out."

Why, Greg? Why shouldn't I pedal too fast? The lights will just come up brighter and the oldie songs will sound louder. That's all you want us to think is happening, isn't it…

Or might it just be, Greg, that if I pedal like crazy, *I* just might travel in time?

The Lone Ranger

◆

Greg Zipprich's friend, Ken, who works with the Sheriff's bomb squad, gave him some .44 caliber bullet casings. He and Greg cast silver bullets in the metal shop foundry and fit them in the casings. Greg carries the silver bullets just like the Lone Ranger but got himself in trouble at the Markham Court Building.

Greg had to go to court for some school business and the metal detector kept going off When he emptied his pockets, out came the silver bullets. The court officers confiscated them and would not give them back. It made no difference that the primer caps had been dented and fired and that there was no powder in the casings. When Greg protested that he was a devoted Lone Ranger groupie, they told him they would talk to Clayton Moore and check it out.

At the time, Clayton Moore was being sued by General Mills. General Mills, maintained that Moore was too old to wear the mask; they now had a new younger guy. It was time for Clayton Moore to stop doing supermarket and Dairy Queens appearances and it was rather unclear if the traditional Lone Ranger or the legal General Mills Lone Ranger was in charge.

As for Greg's silver bullet issue, it seemed lost in a cloud of dust, until Greg appealed to his friend Ken, who was providing body guard protection to Richard Daley. Daley, following in his father's political footsteps, would become Mayor of Chicago, but at the time, he served as the

Illinois State's Attorney. Ken said he'd talk to Daley about getting the Lone Ranger silver bullets back.

In 24 hours, Greg had his silver bullets back.

And as a fitting postscript to Greg's story, Clayton Moore got his mask back. The courts ruled that as long as he could mount a horse, or visit a Dairy Queen, the mask was his.

He was the Lone Ranger.

When Will Winter be Over

◆

My wife, Joan, taught me to gauge the severity of winter by the length of our horses' winter coats. The horses start developing coats for winter in late fall, but I have never been able to tell exactly when winter begins or when it is over.

The date on a calendar? It's a number, that's all.

Fortunately, at school, we had Leo.

Leo Conry is a good man. When the school ran out of money, he was one of the teachers let go with the staff reduction plan. We lost some wonderful and talented teachers to other districts. I miss Leo and his friendship, but I also miss him because he wore penny loafers and in warm weather, he wore no socks.

At Bloom Trail, Leo marked the change of seasons.

"Won't this cold weather ever change? Won't it ever warm up? When will winter end?"

"Have you checked Leo?" I would ask. "Is he still wearing socks?" Because each year at a time only Leo knew, eventually the weather would turn warmer, winter would be over and that morning before he came to work, Leo would have removed his socks.

We would hear Leo's voice on the other side of the cafeteria partition as he waited for his food in the serving line. We would all bend down, look through the bottom opening and check for Leo's socks. It became a standard joke, and one, I admit I originated and perpetuated. But the joke was not at Leo's expense. I never openly made fun of him.

In true scientific fashion, we simply observed his feet each day in early spring under the serving partition. We regarded him respectfully and reverently as our very own ground hog.

Dr. Larry Mazin Gives Me Permission to Change My Life

◆

"You have to learn to handle stress," Dr. Larry Mazin told us at the district teachers' meeting. "Stress will kill you. How effective a teacher will you be when you are dead?"

The program notes said that Dr. Mazin was an educator and a lecturer. He had written a book on stress.

I was stressed out just sitting in the auditorium listening to him, and he was partly to blame.

"So let's talk about ways," he continued, "ways you can *change* the things you do each day to reduce your stress."

At the last minute, Dr. Mazin had requested additional microphones and sound equipment. I had come in early to set the equipment in place and to make the new sound checks.

"I took some time on the plane last night to acquaint myself with this school district."

We couldn't find someone locally? I asked myself. We paid to fly this man out to talk to us? This had better be good.

"And although, I understand you teach children from one of the poorest, most disadvantaged communities in the nation..."

The poorest! my mind interjected. Read your notes over again.

"And although the racial make-up of your district is slightly different than where I come from..."

Slightly? Are your minorities *in* the minority or are your *minorities* the *majorities?*

143

Nope, now I wasn't making sense—even to myself.

Possibly a stress reaction, I thought.

"We all have to remember, 'Kids will be kids.'"

Yes, I agreed, mentally adding, Our kids could chew your kids up into little pieces, spit them out and...

I really wasn't giving this guy, this *Dr.* Larry Mazin, a chance. Being an educator makes you leery of educators.

"Maintaining discipline in the classroom," he preached, "can certainly add to a teacher's stress level, but when you handle your stress effectively, you become a *better* disciplinarian."

Was the guy talking in circles, I wondered, or was there some good stuff here? I had missed the informal breakfast meeting with the guys, and my stomach was growling, interrupting my philosophical musing.

"Today I want to show you how to handle everyday problems that may..."

Two teachers entered the auditorium, their voices raised in argument as they walked toward the front. "You didn't have to go and do that," one of them said.

"I *did* do it," the other teacher loudly replied, "and I'd do it again. I'm not ashamed of what I did. And you had it coming."

"Excuse me!" Dr. Mazin called, "Excuse me! We're having a meeting here."

The argument continued between the teachers, growing in volume. Dr. Mazin left the podium and moved toward the noise. One teacher started pushing the other.

I *think* we are role playing, I thought, but I had to admit, yeah, it was a pretty good show.

"Stop Fighting *Now!*" Dr. Mazin cried. The two teachers stopped yelling and pushing, then looked toward the man.

"This is how I break up a fight," Dr. Mazin said, "and this is how *you* should break up a fight. A lot less stressful, don't you think?" Dr. Mazin was sounding pretty good, lecturing away from the podium with my wireless mike. His booming voice sounded like Charlton Heston's God; no wonder the men stopped fighting.

"You should tell students to stop fighting. You should control the crowd, then send for help. This is the only legal responsibility you have when breaking up a fight. Stop Fighting *Now!*" he shouted again. "Remember those words, those words might be the only words you need."

Right, I thought, he'd have to add a few more words to his incantation if he worked in this district: "Stop! Stop! or I'll twist your head off. Stop! Stop! If you don't stop I'll break the finger I'm holding on to."

No, Dr. Mazin did not understand: some of our kids fought to kill.

Would words have stopped the gunfight at the OK Corral?

Dr. Mazin continued to illustrate his marvelous techniques in handling discipline in the classroom. He invited teachers to misbehave, then dazzled us with his innovative methods of stress-free discipline. People got up and walked around; he quickly got them seated. People began talking during his lecture; he quickly quieted them.

Another fight broke out. "Stop Fighting *Now!*" he called out; he quickly stopped the fight. "Now that I have the group's attention again, I want to continue," Dr. Mazin announced, turning on the overhead projector sitting next to me.

Now we'd see how the man thought on his feet. We were looking at a blank screen. I had all of his transparencies under my coat, and I did not plan to give them back. "Give! Back! *Now!*" I didn't think so.

Dr. Mazin looked at the screen, and then looked at me. "I know you wouldn't take my materials," he said, "but I want to thank you for returning them."

He *knew! How* did he know?

How could you argue with a guy like this? I gave the material back.

"I want to thank you again," he said, completing the job of utterly demoralizing me with kindness, in front of my peers. He was just too good. I behaved myself and listened to the rest of the session.

When the meeting was over, he shook some hands, signed some books, and basked in the glory of his success. I blended in the background, waiting to retrieve the Charlton Heston wireless mic.

When the well-wishers were gone, Dr. Mazin pinched the clip and removed the mic from his lapel.

Just hand me the mic, I thought. You win. I'd taken my lumps and I had earned them and the equation made sense.

Dr. Mazin handed me the mic, then placed his hand on my shoulder. "I had a sports injury last year," he said. "I was playing basketball with some 22 year olds and I pulled a muscle in my leg. My doctor said, 'Mazin, you're 39 years old, what's wrong with you? Don't you know your warrantee has run out?'

"You and I are about the same age," he continued. "How do you break up a fight?"

Why had he singled me out? I wondered as I answered him. "I listened to you very carefully, Dr. Mazin," I said. "You made a lot of sense, but I've had training breaking up fights and restraining students without hurting them. When there's a fight, I usually jump right in there."

Dr. Mazin looked at me for several moments, his hand still on my shoulder. "Fred," he said, looking at my name tag, "I give you permission not to do that any more." His voice was quieter without the microphone, but it echoed slightly in the empty auditorium.

*   *   *

Mazin Reality Check

I thought about Dr. Mazin's advice and described the stress reduction meeting to Joan as we ate dinner.

"He gave me some personal attention," I told her. "It was as if I had a blessing, or a healing."

"Maybe you'll take his advice," she said. "You never listen to me when I ask you to stay out of those fights. Maybe you'll listen to someone else."

"I did listen to him," I replied. "He had some really good things to say."

"Call security when there is a fight," Joan said. "You have five police officers and they're in the building to do that work. It's not your job to get involved."

"You keep forgetting, I *teach*, but I also work with security. I've done this since the day I was hired. I'm usually one of the first people in the building, and I close the place up in the afternoon."

"But you should call security," she said again.

"There are no police officers last hour," I said. "That last hour, I *am* security."

"Listen to the man," she told me. "Don't get so involved." It was a subject we knew well; we usually went around and around on it.

I continued thinking about Dr. Mazin's advice and Joan's concerns the next day. They were both right. All right, then. I would stay out of fights.

That's what I decided—emphatically—as I left the building to supervise afternoon bus dismissal.

In the parking lot, things weren't right. There were more cars waiting than usual, too many kids hanging around, kids who didn't belong. I recognized some of them as gang-bangers who no longer attended school. My friend, Frank Gardner, from the Cook County Sheriff's Office, talked to one of the drivers. His voice was louder than usual. I could hear him from where I perched on the small fold-down step mounted on the side of a bus. Balanced with my head level to the driver's window, I discussed some behavioral problems she was having with her afternoon load of students.

"I'm asking you to leave," Frank told the driver of one car. "That's all I'm doing. I'm asking you to leave."

Frank will handle it, I thought. He handles everything well.

"Screw you, Frank," the driver yelled. "I'm not in school anymore. I don't have to put up with this bullshit."

"I've told you before. You are trespassing on school property. Now I'm telling you, you and your boys, to leave! Now! Before everyone gets arrested."

I glanced behind me. Frank had bent down and leaned towards the driver's window. Always dressed in suit and tie, never a thought to dressing down, Frank looked the professional and role model he was.

"Stay in the car!" Frank demanded, pushing at the door. "Stay in the car! Don't…"

"Fuck you, Frank! Go FUCK Yourself!" I turned again toward the argument.

The driver's door exploded open. I could see the driver's leg, extended. Frank spun backwards; he had been hit by the door. Frank regained his position, then reached for the driver's wrist as the young man pulled himself out of the car. Frank had him now. He had the wrist in the air as if it were a prize. His other hand fished for the handcuffs concealed beneath his suit coat. The cuffs swung toward the target.

He missed!

He never misses, I thought, but the young man was out of the car and standing. With one hand held, and the other free, he pulled back against his captor, then recoiled forward. He shot a fist at Frank's head.

Frank twisted but the blow found its target. The parking lot rang with the crack. The sound pierced through the drone of the bus engine running next to my ear.

I vaulted from my perch to the roadway. "Security!" I called on my radio. "Frank has trouble on the West side." I sprinted to the parking lot.

Frank still had the gang-banger. I jumped on the young man's back, reached over and caught his free wrist. Frank pulled his other arm, spinning us in a circle.

The man screamed, he cursed, kicked, he tried to bite me. I hung on for the ride.

"You're under arrest!" Frank called, as we rolled to the ground. "Stop fighting! You're under arrest!"

"Fuck you, Frank! YOU MOTHERFUCKER," he screamed, but now there were two more police officers grabbing at his kicking feet.

He kicked all the way to the squad car, then battered the door from the inside with his feet.

"Cut it out," one of the officers cried. "You break it, you pay for it." He continued to kick.

Frank re-opened the squad's door and two officers pulled the young maniac back out and laid him down in the street. They cuffed his feet to his wrists and put him back in the squad.

"Anybody in here got a driver's license?" Frank asked the passengers in the car.

"I've got a license, Frank," one of the young men said.

"Show me the license," Frank told him.

"I don't have it with me," the young man said.

"Everyone out," Frank told the group. "Find another way home; I'm calling for a tow truck."

"This is my mother's car," one kid cried out. "I let Charlie drive it, and I have to get it home."

"Tell your mother to pick up her car at the pound on Sauk Trail. Have her call the Steger Police Department," he said.

"Come on, Frank," the kid whined. "I thought we were friends."

"This was quite an afternoon," I said to Frank, as we watched the car-hauler pull the car on board. "Did you ever hear of a Dr. Larry Mazin?" I asked him.

"Who is Dr. Larry Mazin?" Frank asked, rubbing his cheek. "He some kind of dentist?

The Chute-Less Jump

◆

Launch time! Jeffrey Banks spread his arms and jumped off the top of the fieldhouse bleachers. His gym class watched as he flew to the ground. He tucked and rolled, then stood on his one good foot and waved to the crowd.

Why would a sharp kid like Jeff pull a dumb stunt like this? Had he gone crazy?

So when Jeff teetered into class on his crutches the next day, I asked him, "Why did you jump off the bleachers, Jeff? That's a 20 foot drop."

He had a ready answer. "I was bored."

"When your foot heals, will you do it again?"

"No," he said. "Next time I'll jump off the canopy over the school's entrance. It's not as high. Why do you ask?"

"Because you've already shown you are stupid. I just wanted to know how stupid."

"Mr. Anderson," he replied, "I've been trying to get my parents to let me jump out of a plane for two years. I'm practicing!"

Now I understood. Jeffrey Banks was not crazy. He just needed a parachute.

The Idiot

◆

Sometimes a student calls you an "idiot." Sometimes you get called worse. That's part of the teaching package.

So what was so funny about a PE teacher being labeled an *idiot*? Mildly humorous, I thought, or slightly interesting but no big thing.

Yet, whenever this incident was brought up, every other teacher in the PE department went convulsive with laughter.

Then I got it.

It was the last day of school before summer vacation. Terry Murphy, Graphic Arts and PE teacher, related the story.

When Bernie Horvath told his teacher, Mr. Rhyms, "You are an idiot," Rhyms grew angry. His face went red and his hand went for a disciplinary dean's referral. He hadn't gone to college to become a teacher of Physical Education so that a kid could call him an…

Rhyms started to write but stopped. He was stumped. He had to ask his fellow teachers how to spell "idiot."

They all broke out laughing.

They haven't stopped yet.

The Pop Machine Suicide Attempt

◆

Brian Sellers grabbed the money from the pop machine as it was being serviced by the teacher in charge. After a short investigation, Brian's dean found 50 dollars in bills and coins in Brian's locker. Brian got suspended from school for two weeks.

Del Mach, his counselor, contacted me the day before Brian returned to school. "Keep an eye on the kid, Fred," he said. "Watch for signs of depression. He tried to kill himself by dashing his head against his basement wall."

"Was it over the pop machine theft?" I asked.

"Yeah," Del said, "but it was a little more involved than that. Brian's mom felt the kid was out of control, and she took a belt to his backside."

"Perhaps that was the thing to do," I said.

"Maybe," the counselor returned, "but I think the shame of getting caught along with the embarrassment of the whipping from Mom was just too much for the kid to bear."

"I'll watch him," I assured Del. "He was doing all his work up to the time he left school, and I'll spend some time with him to make sure he gets going again."

I watched over Brian in class, but I also noticed that his mother dropped him off at school. She brought him to the main office, and before she left she would kiss him sweetly on the forehead. Unlike many high school kids in that situation, he did not appear embarrassed by his mother's affection.

Sure, I'd keep an eye on Brian. But Brian's mom was doing that and doing a good job of it.

Mom was all right.

And her kid was likely to be all right, too.

Bradoos Mahdoos Whadoos

◆

Secret cryptic massages began to appear on my blackboard. Phrases that made no sense like:

> *Bradoos do*
> *Whadoos do dodo*
> *Mahdoos do whadoos' girls*

Lines like that were sandwiched between the instructions I wrote to my construction trades class. I looked at the words each afternoon as I erased the board.

They would appear the next day during the time I was out in the shop washing up and when the students were returning to the class-room. I didn't have a clue. I needed Sherlock Holmes.

This group of kids had finally mellowed out after a rough first semes-ter. The class had been racially polarized and they accused each other of real and unreal things. We traveled back and forth to the job site on the construction trades bus where they segregated themselves. Black, Hispanic, and White kids sat with their own kind, arranged into five or six clusters.

Some of the White kids complained to me that the Black kids were talking about them. They said that the Black kids were too loud, always laughing and joking. The Black kids said the White kids were critical about their work and sometimes shouted insults at them. The Hispanic kids hung somewhere in the middle of the conflict, physically sat in the middle of the bus and appeared immune to this negative interaction. Once in a while they would explode with some expression of indignation directed at one or the other group.

I rode back and forth to the job site with this "powder keg" on the bus, monitoring and quieting potential problems. At the job site I changed work-team membership, mixed and matched students according to their talents and experiences, and shifted the class's social make-up around during the practical work sessions.

As time went on the groups blended a bit and at least got along better. Some White kids discovered that most of the joking and laughing from the Black kids came from them recounting the Saturday morning cartoons they watched on TV. They memorized and mimicked several favorite shows and loudly ran through the funny lines over and over. Some of the other groups joined in, and things got better.

Just when I thought the class was getting along, the messages began to appear on the blackboard. "You know guys," I started, "I don't know what these words mean, but I know they have *something* to do with racial things. Negative racial comments are not allowed in here. I don't want to hear or see them anymore." I preached on, "I was hoping the class could start to see beyond some of this stuff, and I felt we had come a long way as a group."

"Give us a little credit, Mr. Anderson," one of the Black students said. "Can't you see we *are* all getting along together."

A White student spoke up, "It's just our thing. it doesn't mean anything. We don't have a problem."

I let the matter drop, still unsure of what any of the words meant.

Later in the week I gave the class a "job skill" test from the government.

The test required that the students answer questions as to: Name, Sex, Age and Ethnic background. My instructions from the test booklet were to write a key on the board with each racial group linked to a corresponding number. I wrote the information on the board, gave the test and finished out the regular work day. When the kids left for home I started to erase the board. I stopped the eraser after it hit the first grouping, took the chalk and reestablished what I had first written. The kids had added to the key, and now I knew what everything meant. The board read:

1. American Indian
2. Asian or Pacific Islander
3. Black=BRADOOS-BLACK DUDES
4. Hispanic=MAHDOOS-MEXICAN DUDES
5. White=WHADOOS-WHITE DUDES
6. Other=OTHERDOOS

The code had been broken.
Sherlock Holmes could stay in London.

The Solution

◆

I had kept up with grading papers and had done a pretty good job of recording the mounds of written work generated by a simple assignment: *Read chapter six and seven. Do questions in back of each chapter. Use complete sentences. If you finish, turn in your workbook assignment on page*, etc. etc.

But one day in March, I looked at my desk. I had let myself fall behind in my grading and only a miracle would save me from endless hours of paperwork. Miracles were in short supply at Bloom Trail. I would have to bundle up all the classwork and spend some serious time at home.

Bobbie Diaz came up to the desk. I was sitting down. Bobbie was standing over me. Bobbie said, "I'm sick, I have to go to the nurse." Then he vomited all over the ungraded papers.

I jumped up from the chair. I wrote him a pass. I dumped the papers in the garbage can. Bobbie Diaz gave me the solution of his stomach and the solution to my dilemma. My evening was free.

The Dear Deer Head

◆

Ronnie Tolt hung a deer head in a tree in the school's front yard on Halloween. One of the secretaries was so outraged by the scene when she came to work, that she offered a reward to find out who killed the deer.

It seems a motorist killed the deer and racked up his Chevy station wagon in the process. The secretary paid 50 dollars for this information and got Ronnie Tolt's name in the bargain. Although Ronnie admitted to cutting off the deer's head and putting it in the tree, the police could do nothing. Ronnie said he got the idea from his dad, who as a kid, on Halloween, set mail boxes on fire and exchanged horses between two neighboring stables.

The police said, "Like father, like son."

Wrong Car—Right Car

◆

Paul Pappas, a recent graduate, came back for a visit. "How's it going, Paul?" I asked. "Things okay?"

"I got a new job," Paul replied. "I started on Monday, and for two weeks I'll be working my old job and my new job."

"You're going to end up with a pretty good pay check, working both jobs," I said.

"I'll need it," said Paul. "I moved to the other side of Sauk Village, and some neighbor knocked out two of my car windows."

"Does someone dislike you?" I asked.

"He dislikes the guy I live with, not me," said Paul.

"You will have to put a note on your car that says, *Wrong Car*," I told him.

"Actually," replied Paul, "I put a note on my roommate's car that said, *This is the Car*."

Early Birds

◆

I had a car repaired at the auto shop and left it over night. The next morning, I drove to work in a second car and now had two vehicles at school. Joan told me getting the two cars home was simple. I should drive the first one towards home for several blocks, then run back to get the second car, drive it beyond the first by several blocks, run back to get the first and ellipse my way home.

I told her I would feel like a yo-yo and instead asked Jim Hayden, auto shop teacher, to pick me up the next morning and bring me to work.

Jim goes to work really early. He is the first one in the building. I would have to change my waking habits to be on time, to keep him from waiting; I knew the extra morning time was important for his shop organization.

I went to bed early and set the alarm clock to an hour the alarm hand had never known before. I woke up several times during the night, the way I do if I were going on some early morning fishing adventure, and when the alarm sounded, I jumped out of bed.

I rushed through my early morning chores. I half walked the dog, fed the horses, and let them out of their stalls without the quality time I usually spend with them. I took a speedy shower; only the front of me got wet. I missed a few of my teeth while brushing, but I was waiting at the door early, waiting for Jim's little red Escort. I waited and waited. The predawn birds started to sing. The sun came up and the time got

161

later. Finally Jim pulled into the driveway, well past my usual morning leaving time. He told me he was sorry he was a bit late and we drove to work together.

When Jim dropped me off at the office door I asked if I could pick up his mail. He said he would get his mail later.

I went into the office to sign in, then looked past my name on the sheet. Jim had already signed in and when I checked his mailbox, it was empty.

He had come to work, early as usual, gone to the office as usual, and then to his auto shop, as usual—where he found my car. I imagine it was here he realized he had neglected to pick me up.

Jim had kept quiet about forgetting me because he didn't want me to feel uncomfortable.

Sometimes friends do have secrets.

Show And Tell

◆

"Can I bring my uncle's finger to show the class?" Juan Rivera asked, after I had given my circular saw demonstration. That safety lesson usually brought about a discussion of injuries and cuts, but Juan's request to bring a finger was something special.

"What are you doing with your uncle's finger?" I asked him. "Don't you think he'd mind if you brought part of him to school?"

"He wouldn't mind. He keeps it in our refrigerator," Juan explained.

"Why is he keeping it in your refrigerator," I asked, "and how did he cut it off?" Juan was usually a quiet kid; I knew I'd have to pull the story out of him.

"My uncle got thrown out of a club, you know, a bar, and the bouncer slammed the door on my uncle's hand and cut off his finger."

"But why is he keeping the finger?" I asked.

"He's waiting for someone in the family to die so he can throw it in the coffin for good luck."

"For good luck?" I pressed. "Is that a Catholic thing? A Mexican thing?"

"It's not a Mexican thing," he replied. "It's a *family* thing. Besides, we're Puerto Rican. So what do you think, Mr. Anderson? Can I bring my uncle's finger to class?"

My mind held his question for a moment. I really wanted to see that finger. But, "No, Juan," I had to tell him, "leave your uncle's finger at home in the refrigerator where it belongs."

Charlie One, Two, And Three

◆

"Mr. Anderson, would you walk this young man to his locker?" Miss Lacy, the Dean, asked. "He's new at Bloom Trail and doesn't understand the 'no book pack' policy here at school."

The kid stood before me clutching his new knapsack as if he were about to have his most prized possession taken away.

"I suppose you came from a school where you could carry these things around," I said.

"Yeah," he answered, "how come you can't have 'em here?"

"Guns," I informed him. "We don't want packs around where kids can keep guns."

"That don't make sense," he said. "You can hide a gun down your pants. You don't go around check'n' down people's pants, do you?"

"No, we stay out of people's pants," I said.

"How many cops you got here, anyway?" he asked. "This place is like a prison."

"Four, five, sometimes six," I answered. "All of our security people are off-duty police officers."

"I understand," he said. "My father is a police officer in Crete, and he sometimes works in the school there." His tone had changed, and I could see he was going to cooperate after all.

"Where's your locker?" I asked.

"I don't know," he answered. "Remember, I'm new here."

Fred Anderson

165

"We'll have to go see the locker lady, Mrs. Zuziak," I told him. "She'll assign you a locker. What's your name?"

"Charlie Dunn, the Third," he answered.

"Then your dad is Charlie Dunn, the Second. You must come from a long line of Charlies."

"No," he continued, "my older brother is Charlie Dunn, the First. He's named after my dad, and my other brother is Charlie Dunn, the Second. I am Charlie Dunn, the Third."

"When your parents call, 'Charlie,' how do you know who they're calling? Don't you get mixed-up?"

"I just know that when they call 'Charlie!' and they sound pissed off, they're calling one of my older brothers and not me."

"Is everyone in your family named Charlie?" I asked.

"Uh-huh," he said, "everyone except for my mom and my sister, Charline."

The Limbo Door

◆

Many high schools have Driver Education departments and Auto Shops. I'll bet, though, that Bloom Trail is the only school in the country with a "Limbo Door."

Anthony Kennedy who teaches Driver Education uses my Auto Shop to garage the Driver Ed cars overnight. When I arrive in the morning to meet my first hour class, he has the cars moved out. In the winter, if it has been snowing the day before, there are snow melted puddles and road salt left behind.

I have learned to circumvent the small ponds and have taken on the responsibility of sweeping out the place. When the custodian arrives the night before, the cars are already in place. Although Anthony leaves the car doors unlocked and keys in the ignition, the custodian will not start them and move them outside for a floor sweep.

I have learned to remove my grade book and the papers on my desk. The strong winter winds chase through the shop when Anthony opens the garage door. The wind scatters my work everywhere. I have had to extract some of my bills, invoices and students' written work from those puddles.

I have learned to share the facilities and I appreciate the need to protect the cars leased to the school. However, each night, as I make my last security rounds, checking to see if the school doors are tightly locked, Anthony leaves my garage door ajar, three-quarter down and one-quarter open. When he returns in the first training cars he bends down, enters the shop through the open door, then opens it wide to put away the vehicles.

Here I am, trying to lock up the entire school, and the very room in which I teach is continually exposed to the outside and to unwanted visitors.

I have learned to keep my good nature in this symbiotic relationship by inventing the "Limbo Door."

Each afternoon, as I make my final rounds, I visit my shop one last time. The garage door is open, large enough for Anthony to scramble through. I subtract yet another quarter inch from the pencil marks I have been marking on the wall and reduce the opening just that amount.

Anthony can *still* get through, but the space is getting smaller and smaller. I watch each afternoon from my hiding place in the hallway. He slides under the door and as he squeezes through, I softly sing the "Limbo Song."

Steve And Tom's List

———————— ◆ ————————

"And, when he really gets angry at someone," Steven said, "he pisses in the gas tank."

I was gaining insight into business-customer relationships as I over-heard Steven Biggs talking to Tom Lemmon about the working world.

"What?" I asked. "He does what?"

"Oh, Mr. Anderson," Steven said, "I'm sorry. I didn't know you could hear me."

"That's okay," I told him, "but I want to know what you're talking about." There was definitely a story here.

"We're just talkin' about stuff that goes on at work. Steve was tellin' me about his job at the gas station," Tom explained.

"It's a full service station, Mr. Anderson," Steven explained, "and some of the customers can be real assho…Oops, I'm sorry. They can be real *jerks*."

"Go ahead, Steven," I told him, excusing his language; I wanted him to continue.

"I work with Brandon Martin, and he won't take anybody's shit. When someone jerks him around, you know, is discourteous, he pisses in their gas tank."

"He really does?" I asked in amazement. "What else happens there?"

"He'll take off the gas cap and not put it back," Steven continued. "Then he throws it away. He'll pump eight dollars worth of gas instead of maybe the ten the guy asked for, and keeps the extra money. When he checks the oil, he sometimes keeps their dip stick. And I've even seen him put worms in the gas tank."

Tom worked at a fast food restaurant, and jumped in the conversation. "You should see what they do with the burgers where I work," he said.

"Stop!" I cried. "I can't take anymore. But, do me a favor. Write all this stuff down, so I can look at it later. And at the end, tell me what I can do to keep from getting, *jerked around*."

In the interest of helping to keep the country's economy strong and maintain satisfied consumers everywhere, I present—

Steven's List	*Tom's List*
Gas Station Attendant	*Restaurant Worker*
Urinates in car's gas tank	Puts Visine on food (causes the runs almost immediately)
Keeps dipstick	Uses rotted meat
Goes into restroom, wets toilet paper	Puts live insects on food
Puts worms in gas tank	Won't wash hands after using bathroom
Puts transmission fluid in crankcase	Fries up a roach on the grill to watch it hop

Steven and Tom's Suggestions

1. Pump your own gas or tip at a full service station. At least be courteous.

2. Eat where you can watch the food being prepared.

3. Don't be an asshole.

The Bad Penny

———————◆———————

Roger Duncan, "The Wandering Freshman," was finally evaluated, reclassified, and would soon be out the door. We will only have to put up with this kid roaming the halls for a short time, I thought, looking at his drop notice. Every effort made to get Roger to class on time, or to class at all, had failed. Now that his fate was sealed, this would be his last day.

"Hope things go well for you," I told Roger as I saw him off that last afternoon. "I know you'll like the Alternative School, Roger. Classes are smaller, the day is shorter, and the change could be good for you."

"Sssssee yuh la-later, Mr. Anderson," he called to me while carrying the stuff from his locker. "Sssssee yuh la-later!"

I sat at the security desk the next afternoon. School was over, and the after school activity period had just begun. Roger Duncan stood outside the door, ringing the bell.

Do I really have to let this kid in? I wondered as I walked to the door. I thought we were done with Roger.

"Hi," he called as he walked inside. "Re-mmmm-member ma-me?" He extended a hand. "I'm Roger Duncan...Roger Duncan. I-I u-use to go to sssssschool here."

"I remember you, Roger," I answered. "How are things going? It's always nice to see an old student come back for a visit."

The Invisible Teacher

I am on a ladder, applying a third coat of joint compound to the ceiling. My class is working all around me in this home addition where I have taught them how to hang drywall, tape, then hand-sand the seams. I am dressed in a white paint suit to protect my clothing, and a respirator mask covers my face. A layer of white drywall dust coats my glasses and hides my eyes. The work becomes hypnotic, and I feel I am blending into the wall.

Everyone is into their work. Everyone except for Brian Tully. He has stopped working and is parked in a chair, behind me.

"Brian, why are you so sleepy?" one of the students asks. Brian says nothing; he is probably asleep.

"Brian! Brian! Why are you so sleepy?" the student asks again.

Brian slowly responds, "I'm not gettin' much sleep. I'm workin' eight to two, and gettin' to sleep around three in the morning."

"Are you still washing trucks?" the kid asks him. "What's it cost to wash a truck?"

"It's 43 dollars," Brian answers.

"Do you get tips?" the kid asks.

"Yeah," Brian replies, then pauses. "Last night was good. A driver asked me, 'Who do I pay?' and I told him, 'You pay me,' and he did. I made 43 dollars in one shot."

"I do that at Busy Bee Nursery," another student says, joining the conversation. "If a bag of compost costs two dollars, I load 'em up and collect one dollar a bag from the customer. Everybody's happy."

Brian, a little more awake now, continues, "Those truck drivers at the truck wash are always askin' me if I can get them grass, but they don't deal in small amounts. They want 50 or a 100 dollars worth. Sometimes they have a crack pipe layin' right on the seat. I think what they really want is crack. I thought about sellin' some stuff. The money looks good."

"Don't you guys worry that you might get caught and lose your jobs?" I ask, figuring that it is about time to let them know I am in the room, too.

"No one will figure it out," Brian says. "My dad does that kind of stuff all the time."

I have blown my cover. My students' conversations become less interesting. I think Brian has dozed off again.

Who should be teaching our young people about principles? I wonder, as I finish my work on the ceiling. Parents? Religious leaders? TV? Teachers? Although I haven't found anything in the textbook or class outline about fair play, I try to slip in some ethics lessons. I talk to my students about bids and fair pricing. I stress use of quality materials and doing one's best work.

Thinking about the conversation I've overheard, I wonder if I'm doing my best—if my best is good enough.

But if I can look past Brian dozing behind me, I can see what the rest of the class has accomplished. They have worked hard. They are proud of their new walls and I am proud of their new walls.

And I am proud of my students and the people they can grow up to be.

Bobby's Baby

◆

"Where is Bobby?" I asked, as I counted heads on the roofing project. The weather looked threatening and I needed every kid working hard to get the structure under cover before the rain hit.

"Bobby had to babysit," one of his friends answered. "There was no one to watch his baby, but he said he'd get here as fast as he could."

I couldn't get too mad at Bobby for missing class. His attendance had been good during his girlfriend's pregnancy. They had scheduled her doctor visits after school hours, and when the baby was delivered, Bobby came to class late but directly from the hospital. Red-eyed, with wrinkled, slept-in clothing, he brought the Polaroid pictures of his new-born child, sharing with us his pride and wonder at the baby's birth.

That morning, Bobby fell asleep with his head down on the work-bench, next to the broken rocking horse he had bought at a garage sale and brought to the wood shop for repairs. He snoozed away during my lecture on residential shingle application. I didn't wake him.

But now, here on the roof, I missed the kid. He was a good worker with a hammer and was one of the fastest roofers I had trained. I was relieved to hear someone on the street side of the house call out, "Bobby is here!" but then disturbed to hear the same voice add, "He has his baby with him."

Well, I thought, it doesn't always work out. Rain or no rain, I needed to get out of my crunched up position and take a break. I'd crawl up to the ridge of the roof and down the other side to the ladder. It was time to descend to the ground and meet Bobby's baby.

But I never had the chance to straighten up. Before I got to my feet, Bobby's head appeared over the building's ridge. And then, all of him was standing balanced on the steep roof, his baby riding on his hip.

"I wanted to show my baby the roof," he said to me.

"That is a neat baby," I said to Bobby. "That is one very pretty kid, but we have a safety rule at the high school, Bobby. You can't bring a baby to class and you can't bring a baby on the roof."

"That's okay, Mr. Anderson," he said, "besides, my girlfriend would kill me."

I looked at the thunder clouds rolling in and realized that until we got Bobby's baby down from the roof, I had more things to worry about than the rain.

Mothers And Their Sons

◆

"Hear ye, hear ye, hear yeeee. All rise. The court is now in session. The hon-or-A-ble Judge Marvin L. Wor-ja-HOW-ski, now PRE-ziding. Be seated. No talking, no talking."

It was 20 minutes past the court's posted starting time. Back at Bloom Trail, a substitute teacher sat with my second hour class while I waited, hoping to catch a glimpse of Roosevelt Wilson. If someone molested my child, I thought, I'd cut off his balls.

Yet here I was, called as a character witness by Roosevelt's mother.

"He speaks so highly of you, Mr. Anderson," she had said on the phone. But then she pleaded, "People who know him are our only chance. I need someone who cares about him to talk to the Judge. My Rosy...Roosevelt is...he is still at County, in protective custody. You know how they are down there to sex offenders. I can't raise the bond money." She went on, "When his brother, Cornelius, was in jail for drugs, my aunt died and left me his bail money. No one has died lately."

"I need to know exactly what he did, Mrs. Wilson," I told her. "What did the police report say?"

"He didn't hurt the little girl," she said. "Her mother took her to the ER, and Rosy did not hurt her. But he told the truth to the police, told them exactly what they wanted to know. I taught him not to lie."

Now I looked about the courtroom, hoping to recognize Roosevelt's mom. I'd visualized what she looked like when we talked on the phone, but there was no one in court who fit the picture I had of her. I searched through the faces, one after another, then saw Tina Phillips, a math teacher from our building, entering from the back of the room. I spoke to her as she moved into a seat directly in front of me. "Are you here for Roosevelt?"

"No," she replied quietly, "I'm here for my son." I could tell she didn't want to be bothered by a stranger; she hadn't recognized me.

"James Barker," the Judge began. "Is James Barker in the Court? James Barker? Let the record show that James Barker is not in attendance; issue a warrant for his arrest. Jeffrey Myers," he continued. "Is Jeffrey Myers in the Court? Jeffrey Myers? Let the record show that Jeffrey Myers is not in attendance. Issue a warrant for his arrest. Richard Blake. Is Richard Blake…"

I stared at the back of Tina Philips's head. She sat quietly listening to the judge, then swung her head to look at me. "I didn't recognize you," she whispered. "I'm sorry. I've got a lot on my mind; I'm preoccupied. My son's in custody, and I hope to get him out for Christmas."

"Roosevelt Wilson," the Judge called. "Is Roosevelt Wilson in the Court? Roosevelt Wilson? Let the record…"

"He's in custody, Your Honor," the bailiff announced.

A bell sounded in the lobby.

"The prisoners are being brought up," the bailiff called.

"How have you been, Tina?" I asked quietly. "We don't have the same lunch hour anymore, and…"

"There will be no talking," the bailiff called out. He took several steps towards me and placed his finger abruptly to his lips. Court made me nervous, and now a shot of adrenalin through my veins made the place even more real.

"Bring in Roosevelt Wilson," the Judge ordered. On the other side of an open door, I heard the sound of metal clinking on metal: handcuffs. Then Roosevelt emerged. He held his hands behind him. A uniformed officer followed. Roosevelt raised one hand and waved weakly to a white woman sitting opposite to where Tina and I sat. Roosevelt swung his arm back behind him.

They were taking his cuffs off, not putting them on, I thought, remembering the clinking sound. And that's why I couldn't match Roosevelt to his mother; Roosevelt's mom is a white lady, I thought.

"I haven't had the opportunity to look at the police report, Your Honor," the public defender said. "I'm going to ask for a continuance, sometime in January." Roosevelt stood before the Judge, one hand held the other behind him.

The guards must have told him to stand that way, I thought. I could read the D 0 C letters on the back of his khaki shirt: *Department of Corrections*, I reasoned. It was the same type of shirt worn by the men shoveling the snow that morning from the courthouse walkways.

"Is January 15th all right with you?" the Judge asked the public defender. "And how about you?" he asked the Assistant District Attorney.

"I agree," both of them said. Roosevelt was ushered away. He never said a word.

"Robert Cruz, James Phillips, and Brian Summers," the judge called. "Are these three men in court?"

"They are in custody, Your Honor," the bailiff responded.

"Bring them in," said the Judge.

I heard the rattle of handcuffs again, and three young men were brought toward the bench. Robert Phillips waved to his mother, Tina, and after a short discussion the case was also continued to the other side of Christmas.

Tina turned back and whispered, "He told me this is all over 20 dollars. Last week he watched someone slashed with a razor in prison, and they have threatened his life. He has a wife and small daughter, and he won't be out for Christmas. I'll have to remortgage the house; I'm still his mom."

I had a chance to talk to Roosevelt's mother in the hall before I left, then walked through the lobby and waited my turn at the revolving doors. I stepped into the gray outside.

It was cold on the steps, but not as cold as it was inside the heated building.

Nan Meets Her New Class

———————— ◆ ————————

Only the freshman came to school the first day of the semester. The school board felt it would be a good idea to keep the older kids at home and give the neophytes a chance to find their way around by themselves. The freshman began their day in home room. Teachers passed out their class schedules and asked them to look them over.

"Are there any questions?" Nan Connors asked. "Do you know where you go each period and what your classes are?"

One boy raised his hand and even before she could call on him he shouted out. "I don't want to work on the big stuff!"

"What is the problem?" Nan asked.

"I don't want to work on the big stuff," he repeated.

"What do you mean, the big stuff?" she asked.

"I signed up for Auto Shop," he replied.

Nan walked over to check his schedule.

"I don't want to work on the big stuff," he stated once again.

She looked over his shoulder at his new schedule and studied it for a moment. "Your program says *Introduction to Business*, not *Intro to* **Bus**; you will not be working on big school buses," she explained to him. "You have a business class."

"That's just as bad," the boy said. "I signed up for Auto Shop."

Later that day, Del Mach, the counselor, contacted Nan and informed her a student was coming to class who would not speak.

"Is it that he can't speak or that he *won't* speak?" she asked Del.

"I'm not sure," he said to her. "I just know that his records from the upper grade center state that he would not speak, and that you should not expect him to reply to questions in class. I'm sorry," he continued, "I'm away from my desk and can't remember his name."

"How will I know who he is?" Nan asked.

Del laughed and replied, "Just listen for someone in the class who's not talking. But seriously, I'll get right back to you with his name."

And so he did. He gave her the student's name before the class met that day, so when the group was seated, Nan knew who he was, the boy who would not speak.

A few minutes into the class period, the boy who would not speak made a sound. Actually he made a series of sounds that to Nan represented speech. He had only been in her class a short while and already he was talking to her, loudly and in front of the whole room.

"I don't want to be in your fuckin' class," he said.

"What did you say?" she asked, not quite believing her ears.

"I don't want to be in your fuckin' class," he replied again.

Nan raised her arms and looked upward.

She acknowledged the wondrous event and quietly said to herself. "It's a miracle, a wonderful miracle."

Voice From the Past

◆

Barbara Watson approached Nan Connors on the "Parents Back-to-School Night." "Mrs. Connors, you might not remember me, but I had you for my teacher. My daughter, Brenda, has you now."

"I remember you, Barbara," Nan replied. "How have you been?"

"I've been fine, thank you. You know, I was pregnant when I was in your class. I was carrying Brenda."

"Well, then," Nan said, "Brenda should do well. Some of the material is the same, and she should remember the sound of my voice."

Five Short Chapters About Roger Commings

◆

LOGIC

Roger Commings was chronically truant. His punishment?
The school suspended him for three days.

ROGER'S STATEMENT OF INTENT

"I have to pass the second semester. I will be in school from now on," Roger Commings declared.

I QUESTION REALITY

"I bet you won't," I said, looking at Roger's grades and absences recorded in my grade book.

ROGER'S REAFFIRMATION

"Oh, yes, I will…

CONDITIONS AND EXCEPTIONS

"Except for Senior Ditch Day or maybe a really sunny day where I'll have to go to the beach, and, oh yes, a week from this Friday. I have to do some stuff. I found out who messed up my car and I have to do a number on him."

On Friday, Roger was truant.

Tuesday, A Slow Day for Drew

◆

I once watched my friend, black belt judo instructor and science teacher, Drew Wickham, fight in a judo demonstration. He took on one opponent after another, and after an hour he was undefeated and still standing.

So it was something of a surprise to learn Drew was as mortal as the rest of us. It was Tuesday when a girl in his science class spread Krazy Glue on his chair.

She waited for Drew to sit down.

He did.

Usually, Drew has all of the moves, but glued to his seat, he didn't move too fast that Tuesday.

I Close the School

──────────◆──────────

It had been snowing all day and snowing the day and night before. The high winds continued to drift snow over the roads leading to the high school. The parking lot was a mess and the temperature was dropping into the sub-zeros. Chicago schools had closed their doors that day as did a good number of suburban districts that surround us. But true to form, and unlike the neighboring schools, we were open for business.

I left the building that afternoon for a meeting at the district office. All day I heard the murmurings of students and staff: would school be open the next day?

"We never close," I remarked. "The people who run this place come from pioneer stock. Some schools close up after a flake of snow, but I bet we will stay open."

I rocked my car out of a snow drift, drove the several miles to the district office and plowed into another drift. Attending this meeting was almost as stupid as going to work the next morning, I thought as, cursing the pioneers and their stock, I pushed the snow away with the car door and stepped into the drift.

If I had the power I'd close school tomorrow because of the weather. The snow was finding its way into my low cut shoes.

The district office had changed its exterior doors.

The same "ring for assistance" bell mounted at our building was installed in the hallway leading to the office doors. Locked entrance doors, video cameras, intercoms and security personnel, definitely a sign of our times, I reflected. We've gone to a fortress concept, protecting us from savages, bandits, irate parents—and from the very students we are trying to teach. Just anyone can't come in here, I thought as I stated my business.

"I've come to meet with Mr. Lauritsen."

"He's expecting you," the call box answered. "Come right in."

Just like Burger King, I thought as the door lock clicked open.

"I'll have some french fries," I said, immediately realizing that the joke must be really old.

"I'll get you a cup of coffee," the receptionist said, "but no fries."

I walked into Mr. Lauritsen's office.

"What's on your mind, Fred?" he asked, "It's good to see you."

"I came to talk about my retirement," I said, "but I think I can simplify the meeting. I'd like to change the topic, and as one of your most experienced geezers, tell you to close the school tomorrow."

"We're working on that," he said, and with that, the phone rang.

Ron Patton, the superintendent, was on the line and asked for Lauritsen's input on closing school. Lauritsen looked at me and asked, "What do you think?"

"Close school," I said, and so they did.

When I returned to the high school, the place was a ghost town. The people who usually hang around were gone; they had looked at the weather and headed for home.

Mr Krygier, our principal, Sue Condon, his secretary and Mr. and Mrs. Deakin were trying to set up an antiquated answering machine to announce Friday's school closing. They had struggled with the system for over an hour, had finally gotten it to work, and were developing the perfect announcement for the occasion.

Mr. Krygier announced: "Due to the inclement weather, school will be closed on Friday and will reopen on…"

The announcement was perfect. He spoke in a clear, concise manner and the switchboard channeled all incoming calls to the machine.

We put on our coats; the long day was over. Sue made one last call to check the equipment.

"You'll have to go back and change the announcement," she said. "There is something wrong."

I called the number from the pay phone in the hall and listened to Mr. Krygier's message one more time—and all the way through: "Due to the inclement weather, school will be closed on Friday and will reopen on…June 17th!"

Up to this time I had felt proud of myself; I was single-handedly responsible for closing school, but Mr. Krygier had gone one better. His announcement closed the school for the rest of the year.

That's real power.

The Fugitive

◆

I found the kid outside the school building, hiding in a pit between the loading dock and the dumpster. He was facing away from me and I quietly stole up behind him. I watched him peek over the dumpster, then drop down into the pocket of his hiding place, evidently watching for the school's security officers.

The temperature was just above freezing. It had started to rain, and I could see that his head and the shoulders of his jacket were wet.

"How long are you planning to stay out here in the rain?" I asked him.

Startled, he turned and faced me. His eyes were at the level of my shoes. "I'm going to stay here until school is over and then I'm going to get on a bus," he answered.

"Why are you out here and not inside the building?" I asked. "Have you been suspended?"

"Yes," he answered, "but I haven't been in the building all day. I stayed outside the whole time."

"I bet your parents don't know you were suspended," I said. "I bet you came to school and are trying to get through the day to ride the bus home."

"Yes," he said, shivering. "Are you going to turn me in?"

I bent down to read the name on his ID. "Robert Benson, come inside and we'll both get out of the rain," I told him, avoiding his question; I didn't know what I was going to do.

My decision should have been simple. All I had to do was key the radio I was carrying. One of the security officers would come outside, take Robert to his dean, and further complicate the kid's day.

But I brought him inside to get warm and dry. I was interested in finding out what made this kid tick.

I found an empty classroom for him to sit. "If you can stay put," I told him, "maybe we can get you through the day without being found. I'm going to ask you to do one thing. Here is some notebook paper and a pencil. Write down what was on your mind this morning when you came to school. Did you think you could get away with this? Tell me what you wore and if you prepared for this weather."

He looked at me, puzzled. I wondered if he thought I were nuts.

I brought him a sandwich and a glass of milk from the cafeteria, and periodically came back to check if he was still there. When school was over, he escaped into the mass of students leaving for home. He left behind the pencil and this note for me.

This story is his.

So are the grammar and spelling.

Robert's Story

I dressed in normal clothes, a swetshirt jeans sneekers and a jean jakit. I pland on walking to school, hiding outside as long as need be, then taking the bus home.

Yes, I thought that I would be abel to get away with it. I am a very sneekey person who gets away with a lot. I was suspended 2 days out of school for faling asleep in I.S.S. (in school suspension). I was in I.S.S. becaus I was caut truent Thursday the 20th of Febuary whiel I was out-side smoking.

Getting caught fels like being stuck between a rock & a hard spot. I've had alot of close cales, but to day you were the only one to catch me.

Thank for not busting me. I ow you a lot, so if you ever need a favor let me know.

I had wanted to find out what made this kid tick. In the limited time I had spent with him I learned he was definitely sneaky. I had learned that he had no business falling asleep in any class, particularly a class that taught spelling.

I had learned that he appreciated someone who asked him in out of the rain.

The Smoke Lodge

◆

Jimmie Eubus's attendance had been terrible. This talented kid's grade point average was in the toilet. But lately he had been coming to school.

"Jimmie," I said to him, "this is great. You're coming to class and if you keep it up you just may pass."

"I've had perfect attendance now for two weeks," he announced. "I've straightened some things out."

"Did you go to church and find Jesus," I asked him, "or maybe Buddha or Mohammed?"

"It was something like that," he answered. "I went to North Dakota and my grandfather made me sit in the smoke lodge. He wouldn't let me out for four hours and I had some time to think about myself."

"What was it like in there?" I asked, genuinely interested.

"It was low to the ground, small, hot, and smoky with a tea kettle or something steaming away. Mostly," he said, "it gave me lots of time to think."

"What did you think about?"

"Just that I wanted to graduate and move on with my life," he answered.

Eric Smith was standing nearby, listening to the conversation. "How 'bout drugs? Did you get any drugs? Were there drugs?"

Jimmie looked at him, paused for a moment, and then told him. "It wasn't about drugs, Eric. It was a smoke lodge and I was in there thinking."

Genderbenderelia Goes to the Ball

♦

I stopped and looked at Jeremy's project as he worked at his bench. "It is a shame you aren't under 21," he said to me.

"Yes, it is a shame," I said to him, "but getting older isn't too bad."

"I didn't mean that," he said. "If you were under 21, you could come to the *Starlight Teen Club*. I'm going to cross dress tonight."

"Do you expect any problems, or will people leave you alone?" I asked, surprised that we were talking about this subject.

"Yeah," he said, "things will be cool. I'll have no problem."

On Monday I revisited Jeremy at his work station. "How was the weekend?" I asked.

"Not too good," Jeremy said.

"How did the cross dressing go?" I asked. "Did you have trouble getting into your heels?"

"It didn't go too well," he answered. "They charged me five dollars to get in and later asked me to leave."

"Were you causing trouble?" I asked.

"No," he answered. "The management said they were having too many complaints. They asked me to leave."

"I thought Dennis Rodman and the clothes he wears would have paved the way," I said.

"So did I," he returned. "If Rodman had been there, I might have gotten my five dollars back."

Old Man at the Door

---◆---

I still have that spring in my step, I thought as I walked to Terry Murphy's classroom to deliver a phone message. I can out-work and out-climb any kid in my Construction Trades Class. I can still lift more than any of my students. I went on and on in my mind, being honest enough to qualify it with, Outlift any of them *except* for Joseph Nunez.

Joseph, at 17, ran his own landscaping business. He could boost two bundles of shingles up the ladder on his shoulders. He could lift a Buick.

I knocked on Terry's locked door, still marveling how young I was, even after 33 years of teaching.

And here I was, ready to retire.

Me, retire?

One of Terry's students came to the door and looked at me through the glass. "Mr. Murphy," she called to Terry, "there's an old man at the door."

Me.

Retire.

Printed in the United States
3813